Triple 'O' Seven

TRIPLE 'O' SEVEN

by
Ian R. Jamieson

Talonbooks • Vancouver • 1985

published with assistance from the Canada Council

Talonbooks
201/1019 East Cordova
Vancouver
British Columbia V6A 1M8
Canada

This book was typeset by Resistance Graphics in 12 point Baskerville and printed in Canada by Hignell Printing Ltd.

First printing: March 1985

Canadian Cataloguing in Publication Data

Jamieson, Ian.
    Triple 'O' seven

ISBN 0-88922-223-1

I. Title.
PS8569.A44T74 1985   C813'.54   C85-091137-0
PR9199.3.J35T74 1985

FOREWORD

The information contained herein is a parody which, by definition, is a humorous or burlesque imitation of a literary work. All the characters and events depicted are real and alive in the writer's imagination. This is the first in a series of books which will take the reader into an array of totally bizarre and wild plots conceived by the villains, and tell of the thwarting of their dastardly schemes by our hero,
TRIPLE 'O' SEVEN.

Whether young or old, sane or slightly crazy, everyone will laugh at the antics of Triple 'O'. So wherever you are reading this, enjoy! And remember: the first laugh belongs to me because you just paid for this book.

Regards,

Chapter One

LONDON, 1942

The woman screaming and writhing on the sterile steel table was named Anastasia Klause. She was twenty-nine years old and very beautiful. Her place of origin was somewhat unclear; it was believed her place of birth was Switzerland, but her formative years had actually been spent within the city walls of Moscow.

Anastasia was a spy, a double agent by profession, skilled in all aspects of espionage. At this particular moment, however, she found herself helpless, and it was all she could do to keep herself under control. Her screams made the continuous waves of pain easier to withstand, but the pain was becoming unbearable. Dr. Veckoff looked at her over the steel rims of his glasses, his red pig-like eyes running up and down her body. She was swollen quite badly. He noticed rivulets of sweat running from the damp fair hair onto the nape of her neck as she strained against the shackles at her wrists and ankles. She had bitten her lip and small droplets of blood were mixing with the sweat. He had a grudging respect for her—she had been in agony for almost three hours now and still had not given him the name he wanted.

"The name, Anastasia, the name. Give me the name," he demanded, for what seemed like the hundredth time.

Anastasia, her mind reeling with the pain, dimly heard Dr. Veckoff ask again for the name. God-damn it! she thought, how much longer will this go on? Another burst of pain, another scream. I must keep a hold on myself.

She needed something to focus on, in order to maintain control. As difficult as it was, she opened her eyes and looked into the ugly pock-marked face of Dr. Veckoff. She cursed herself again for the stupidity that had led her into this predicament. Both M15 and the fledgling S.P.E.C.T.O.R. control organizations had given her specific instructions on how to avoid this situation, and she had let it happen. She clenched her fists until her nails dug into the flesh of her hands. She had lost all track of time since the ordeal had begun under the close scrutiny of Dr. Veckoff. Oh yes, the well-known, horrible Dr. Veckoff, a true professional.

Dr. Veckoff had two able assistants. It was they who had tied her wrists and ankles. As the pain seared through her body, her nails broke through the skin of her hands. Blood spurted and dripped to the floor. She looked up at the other two people in the room. The first was a woman somewhere in her forties. Anastasia had never seen or heard of her, but from the way she assisted Dr. Veckoff, she knew that the woman had been here before. It was obvious they were experts: each knew each other's role in this assault on her body, and only the smallest amount of dialogue passed between them.

The woman was ugly and built like a tank. Her face had a sickly grey pallor to it and folds of flesh hung from her face reminding Anastasia of an old British bulldog. The skin was dry and cracked and her thin grey lips compressed into a bizarre, ghastly white line every time Anastasia screamed. The woman seemed cold, deadly cold. Her small unblinking snake-eyes never left Anastasia's face. It was as if she was looking for the first sign of weakness.

Another shudder passed through Anastasia as her eyes found Dr. Veckoff's other assistant. If the woman was ugly, and she was, her perfect mate would have been this man. He was thin, almost anorexic. The single bare light bulb hanging from the low ceiling cast nasty shadows over his features. His eyes were so sunken and his cheeks so sallow that he looked like something from a freak or horror show. To add to the effect, his hair grew in clumps from a balding head. His slightly protruding teeth were yellow and decayed and his stinking breath filled the room. The lips curled back from the rotten teeth as he glanced quickly at Dr. Veckoff. He sensed it was nearly time to bring all the pain Anastasia was going through to an end. Dr. Veckoff, standing a few feet away, nodded in reply.

Anastasia could see the excitement in the rodent-like assistant. He was now covered in a thin film of sweat, and his body started to give off a foul odour, like that of a dead animal. He reached for a small black leather bag perched on the sterile steel trolley close to Anastasia's head. She watched with horror as he pulled out two items. The first was a syringe filled with a yellowish liquid. He pulled the cap from the one-inch needle and held the point of it up towards the light bulb. He then removed the air bubbles by squirting some of the liquid from its point. Again, the lips curled back from those rotten teeth, and he licked his lips in anticipation. A dribble of spittle fell from his upper lip onto his chin. He wiped it away with the back of his hand. The second item from the bag was a folded, flat leather case. With what seemed like immense pleasure, he opened the case in front of Anastasia's face. She suddenly knew what they were going to do to her and her eyes widened with terror.

From the case, Veckoff's assistant extracted one of a dozen different-sized razor sharp scalpels. He held the chosen one up to the naked light bulb and twisted it slightly. Its honed edge caught the light and glistened. Satisfied with his inspection, he passed the instrument to Dr. Veckoff. Veckoff drew close.

"Give me the name, Anastasia," he whispered. "Tell me the name."

The only response from Anastasia was a full-throated scream as another wave of pain coursed through her swollen body.

"I think it's time I brought this little episode to an end," muttered Dr. Veckoff. He held the scalpel up to the light as his assistant had done, checking the fineness of the edge. He gave one last look at Anastasia and quickly and expertly pushed the point of the scalpel into the most sensitive area of Anastasia's body.

Anastasia gave one final wrenching scream before she lost consciousness. In the distance could be heard the faint sounds of the air raid sirens signalling yet another attack by the Luftwaffe, about to drop their cargo of death on the frightened citizens of London.

•

Anastasia Robena Klause had been born twenty-nine years ago. Her parents were wealthy landowners who associated with the royal families of Europe. She found herself equally at home with the peasants who worked the land or with the titled in their aristocratic homes and castles. She had a gift for languages that enabled her to speak several fluently, and this, coupled with an extraordinary beauty inherited from her fine looking parents, resulted in Anastasia being much sought after by the high-living bachelors of

European society.

She discovered, however, that everything seemed shallow and without purpose. It was through a chance attendance at a politically-oriented youth meeting that she found her true vocation. The group, striving for political change, advocated violence and sabotage to obtain its goals and gain recognition for their cause.

From the very first bridge she blew up, Anastasia knew that this was what life had ordained for her. The incredible rush of excitement, the adrenalin pumping through her body, nerves jangling with danger—this was what she craved. She threw herself heart and soul into perfecting the arts of sabotage, self-defence, assertiveness, disguise, deception, and so on; and in doing so, inadvertently fulfilled all the prerequisites for being a good spy.

Through secret channels known only to such people in that clandestine but omnipresent world, she was approached by a fledgling terrorist organization headquartered in Moscow, known as S.P.E.C.T.O.R. The Society for the Promotion of Espionage, Conquest, Terrorism, Obstinacy and Revenge would, over the years, come to play an important role in shaping world events.

Anastasia's one fault was that she could be swayed very easily by any moderately good salesman. S.P.E.C.T.O.R. successfully recruited her by offering her the freedom to use her own judgment in all situations and a complimentary set of steak knives. She did what she liked when she liked. There were some very highly qualified people in the ranks of the early S.P.E.C.T.O.R. organization and she felt pride in belonging to a group of top professionals.

To Anastasia, espionage was the ultimate game. If you lost, you were dead. You not only had to have the basic skills to survive, but in order to win you had to have an innate sense of the game that set you apart from the rest of the operatives. Only this sixth sense could make you a winner, and Anastasia had it. After nine successful years operating in a number of hot beds of intrigue, she was assigned to England. It was here that a sequence of events eventually led to the predicament she was now in.

Her mission had been to gather as much information as she could on the Crypton Decoder that the British were using to decipher German radio signals. The decoder was housed in a top secret establishment known as Bletchly Park Manor, situated in one of the prettiest places in the Berkshire Hills just south of London.

Anastasia knew that she had done everything right but, being the professional she was, she also knew that something was going wrong. Her sixth sense told her that she was being watched, but she didn't yet know by whom. What really puzzled her was how fast she had been spotted. Only two weeks in the Bletchly area and somehow she knew that her cover was blown. Why hadn't she been arrested?

As one day passed into another, she grew more and more fearful, almost to the point of abandoning her mission. To try to appear casual she dressed herself up and went to the Crown and Anchor public house to have a few drinks and mix with the local townspeople.

The old pub, built sometime in the seventeenth century, had a very warm decor and good ambience. It was larger than most of the traditional local pubs and the place was packed. A thick wall of smoke hung from the ceiling. A large group of sailors were singing around a piano in one corner. Privates, officers, and villagers were standing shoulder to shoulder and not giving an inch as Anastasia fought her way to the bar. Just as she reached her destination, an attractive woman and a young soldier vacated two of the bar stools. As Anastasia sat down, a tall, good looking man with steel grey eyes sat down beside her. She gave him a quick appraisal and liked what she saw. Wide shoulders, narrow waist and obviously well-muscled under his loose fitting jacket. He gave her a look of approval and smiled, showing even white teeth, but said nothing.

"Good evening, folks, what can I get you to drink?" asked the genial bartender.

"I can't speak for the lady, but I will have a vodka martini, on the rocks with a twist of lime; stirred, not shaken." He looked as Anastasia questioningly.

"That sounds fine. I will have the same," she replied.

The drinks came very quickly, and the man sitting next to Anastasia paid for both of them.

"Thank you very much," she said, sipping her drink. "This is delicious. With whom do I have the pleasure of drinking, this evening?"

The man looked at her with an amused smile on his face. His eyes seemed to bore into hers. He sipped his drink and took his time answering. When he did, she noticed a very faint Scottish accent.

"My name is Blond. James Blond. Lieutenant James Blond." Again he gave her that smile of amusement.

Anastasia saw him give another questioning look but before she could answer, he spoke again.

"I know who you are. You're Anastasia Klause. Spy for S.P.E.C.T.O.R. and currently on assignment to find out about the Crypton Decoder." His eyes still looked directly into hers and that damned smile of his was infuriating. A rush of adrenalin spurred her to immediate action. Turning away from him ever so slightly, she braced her foot against the bar-rail. Pretending to raise the drink to her mouth, she swung the glass in a vicious arc at Blond's head.

Anticipating the move, Lieutenant Blond leaned backwards from the bar stool, bumping a soldier and spilling the man's drink. Even so, Blond felt the glass break and cut the skin just over his right eyebrow.

He looked at Anastasia, still with a smile on his face. "Well, that really is not very sociable." The disturbed soldier glanced at his empty glass in mute sorrow, took one look at Blond, and swung at him. As the great fist of the soldier started on its way, a lightning-fast chop to the throat and two fingers in the solar plexus rendered the soldier a crumbling hulk. He fell to the floor, gasping for beath. Two sailors directly behind Anastasia seized the opportunity to take a swing at one another. One of them missed his target and rocked Anastasia instead. Having put up with almost three weeks of unbearable tension, Anastasia suddenly exploded into a rage. As she dispatched the two sailors, bedlam broke out in the Crown and Anchor Pub. Chairs, tables, bottles and glasses flew across the room as some two hundred locals and soldiers got into the spirit of the event. The pressures of wartime are great, and even such stout hearts as these required relaxation. Blond pulled Anastasia aside as a chair narrowly missed her face. Immediately, Blond was seized by a giant of a man who seemed intent on holding him forever. It didn't seem to matter where Blond hit him, it hurt his hand more than the man.

Anastasia, wondering why this man had saved her from the flying chair, now looked at him held up against the wall in front of the towering hulk. God, she thought, he was handsome, and gave him another admiring look. It would be interesting to see how he handled the giant.

The hulk aimed a tremendous right hand at Blond's head. The huge fist missed by a hair's breadth and went right through the wall, sending a spray of plaster and lath over Blond's jacket. Seeing this, and against all her training, Anastasia went to the aid of the man who it seemed could determine whether she lived, or died at the end of a noose for espionage. With her long golden hair flying, she rushed in between the two men. The huge man pulled his fist from the wall and stepped backwards.

"Why don't you pick on someone your own size, you big lump of dog shit?" Anastasia inquired.

14

The big man looked at her. "Get out of my way, Lady," he snarled.

"Don't think of me as a lady," said Anastasia.

Lieutenant Blond looked at the confrontation between the big man and the beautiful woman a third his size. It would be interesting to see how she handled him.

"Oh, yeah? If you're not a lady, what are you then? A man?" In the department of great wit and gay repartee, this lout was ten inches short of a foot, but his comeback seemed to strike his funny bone and he roared with laughter. Anastasia looked at Blond and then brought her foot up with all the power she could muster, landing it squarely in the man's groin. The brute doubled up and his laughter turned into gasping and wheezing.

"I told him not to think of me as a lady," said Anastasia as she turned to Blond.

The whole pub was now close to total demolition. Over the din of the fighting, a siren could be heard.

"Let's get out of here," said Blond, gently holding her elbow and steering her through the mass of fighting bodies. "I think the M.P.'s are on their way, and we certainly don't want to be detained by them, do we?"

Anastasia did not answer. For some inexplicable reason, she allowed herself to be led out of the Crown and Anchor. It was as if this man had an aura about him in which she felt secure, something she had never felt with any man before, let alone one that could determine whether she would live or die.

Gaining the street, they quickly climbed into Lieutenant Blond's Jaguar and drove off, out of Bletchly, heading towards Oxford. They passed two jeep loads of Military Police going in the opposite direction, and waved as they passed.

No words were spoken as the car hurtled along the narrow country roads at breakneck speed. The minimal light from

15

the car's blacked-out headlights barely allowed Lieutenant Blond to see the road, but there was a full, bright moon and the sky was clear. Anastasia looked at the strong profile of the man sitting next to her. He was intent on driving the Jaguar and seemed to enjoy the thrill of the high speed and the wind lashing his face.

The car turned onto what looked like a private drive. A few short twists and turns later, with gravel crunching under the tires the car came to a halt in front of a large country manor. Anastasia, using her knowledge of time and direction formulas, placed the house at about eight miles south of Oxford; by her estimation she was on the outskirts of Culham, a small village nestled on the north bank of one of the upper reaches of the Thames.

She followed Lieutenant Blond into the manor and entered a comfortably furnished sitting room. She watched as Blond walked across the room to the fireplace and touched one of the tiles. The fireplace and a section of the wall moved backwards and then slid sideways to reveal a passageway of descending stairs. As soon as they passed through it, the wall closed behind them.

Reaching the bottom of the stairs, they went down a long, narrow dimly lit corridor. A steel door at the end slid aside with a whisper. They entered a large, bright room that bustled with activity. There must have been some twenty men and women in the room poring over maps, typewriters and what looked like a bank of radio receivers. They continued through a heavy wooden door which opened up into a small office. Lieutenant Blond aimed his trilby hat at a coat rack. It swung through a graceful arc and landed perfectly on one of the wooden pegs.

"Hello, Miss Mummypenny," said the Lieutenant. He addressed a smiling woman whose eyes shone at the sight of him. It was obvious to Anastasia that Miss Mummypenny adored him. She felt an unfamiliar pang of jealousy.

16

"N is expecting you, James. Go right in. What happened to your head?"

Blond touched the swelling on his forehead where Anastasia had caught him with her drink glass. "Oh, this. One too many dry martinis," he said, smiling ruefully and casting a quick glance at his companion. Miss Mummypenny raised her eyebrows and Blond opened the door and led Anastasia into a very large, luxurious office.

The room smelled of rich leather. Indeed, all the furniture was upholstered in leather. Most of the chairs were a deep red colour with what looked like brass studs. The desk was huge and black as ink. Anastasia wondered what kind of wood it was. Papers were scattered over the desk and a bank of telephones was ready for use. Obviously, an intelligence organization's headquarters, but which one? At no time in her briefings had she ever heard anything about an organization with its headquarters in this area of England.

The man behind the desk, she supposed, was N. He had a lot of grey hair and looked distinguished, although his maturity seemed much greater than his years. His eyes were dark and very intense. Anastasia placed him in his middle forties. With a crisp movement of his hand that made Anastasia start, he reached for one of the telephones.

"Miss Mummypenny, hold all calls until further notice." He rose from behind the desk and offered his hand to Blond. "Good to see you again, James." They shook hands, and N turned to Anastasia. "Miss Anastasia Klause, I trust that you have already been formally introduced to Lieutenant James Blond. I'm known as N in this organization. It seems that James has brought you here a little earlier than expected." He looked at Blond who casually shrugged and gave that same relaxed smile that Anastasia found infuriating, yet fascinating. He extended his hand to her and she shook it, noticing its coolness. "You were not supposed to be here until tomorrow. No matter, let's get down to

17

business." He sat down again behind his desk and pulled a file from one of the many stacked in front of him.

"Miss Klause, in order to save time, I'll tell you that we have a very extensive file on you and have watched your activities over the last nine years, including your recent association with S.P.E.C.T.O.R. We are very impressed with your work. Being in a similar line of work ourselves, we recognize talent when we see it. However, individual talent, while certainly being a prerequisite of success as a spy, also has to be backed up by a first class organization, and quite frankly, and objectively speaking, that is where we have a distinct advantage over any other spy organization in the world." N paused and offered her a cigarette, which she took. He lit it with a desk lighter. Apparently Blond did not smoke as he was not offered one by N.

"What I am saying, of course, is mostly rhetorical. You can either accept it or not. I do not want to get into a discussion with you regarding the merits of different organizations. The reason that you are here, Miss Klause, is that we wish to enlist your help for a project which requires your special talents. We really don't care who you work for or what your political ideology is, we just require your assistance for a brief time."

"And if I refuse?" asked Anastasia, trying to hide her surprise and gain some time to weigh all the options.

"If you refuse, then I'm afraid that I will have to ask James to shoot you on the spot. James, do you have your pistol?"

Anastasia looked at Blond, who was already attaching a silencer to his pistol.

"You didn't for one moment think that we would let you walk through our headquarters if you had any kind of choice, did you?" said N.

"Whatever happened to the famous English justice system? I thought that even spies got to have a trial."

"That used to be the case," replied N, "but this is a new and very flexible department which has given selected agents a double 'O' prefix to their code number. Blond is '007'; the prefix gives him the right to kill at any time, with no questions asked."

"As one professional to another," said Blond, "I think it goes without saying that I will shoot you without hesitation if you refuse, and I know you will understand." Again, that infuriating smile as he played with her life.

N interrupted. "I should perhaps mention, that we are prepared to offer you not only your life, but this attractive set of steak knives." From a drawer in his desk, N withdrew a teak case and flipped up the top, revealing as fine a set of cutlery as Anastasia had ever seen. "In addition, they never need sharpening," he concluded.

Anastasia stared straight ahead and gave her answer. "As a professional, I can tell you that I would love to work with you. On one condition. I work with Lieutenant Blond. If that's not acceptable, then pull the trigger." She was pleased at the surprise that registered very slightly in Blond's eyes. He looked inquiringly at N.

"I would like both of you ready to parachute into France within the hour. James, you can brief Miss Klause on the assignment." His decision was also a dismissal for them both. As they left the office, Anastasia could not help but overhear N as he called to James. "Oh, James, kill Miss Klause if she doesn't perform."

The small Lysander plane skipped across the English Channel no more than fifteen feet above the choppy surface. Their faces blackened, Blond and Anastasia readied their parachutes and Blond, shouting into her ear over the noise of the engine, filled in the last details of the mission.

Apparently, a small multinational group had joined up

with French Resistance and was now being retrained and reorganized as the Allies moved their way through Europe. Anastasia's knowledge of languages and technical expertise in sabotage and in the training of such people had placed her as one of a dozen people on a short list compiled for N. Blond had tracked down two of the others only to find that they had been killed shortly before he could recruit them. Another had refused. Anastasia was his fourth try.

The rag-tag resistance had to be coordinated fast. Key bridges had to be blown up to disrupt German troop movements, and delay the shipments of supplies they so desperately needed. The problem was communication. Anastasia would be very useful as Blond's translator and chief assistant.

The pilot had been hopping over the trees and fields of the French countryside for some time now. He turned in his seat and signalled that he was close to the target and was going up to give them enough height to jump.

The plane climbed steadily towards the full moon, finding very little cover in the few scudding clouds. Suddenly it was violently shaken by shells ripping through the light wing structure on the starboard side. Blond and Anastasia looked on as one of the Luftwaffe plane's bullets ripped through the pilot's flight jacket and penetrated his heart, killing him instantly. The pilot slumped back, clinging to the joystick with a death grip and sending the plane into a near vertical climb. The engine began to cough and sputter. Blond sprang into action. Reaching forward and mustering his strength, he pulled the rigid pilot away from the controls and back over the seat. Anastasia deposited the body unceremoniously on the floor and Blond struggled into the seat. The engine of the Lysander was now screaming with effort and stalled just as Blond took over the controls.

"Now then, where's the Hun?" said Blond, as he fought to put the plane into a controlled dive, simultaneously trying to revive the engine. Incredible, thought Anastasia. He makes jokes. Then, realizing Blond was serious, she shook her head in disbelief.

"Are you crazy?" shouted Anastasia through the noise. "This plane doesn't carry any weapons. You're not going to fight him?"

"Hold tight," said Blond, his grin replaced by a grim mask of concentration.

The plane was now plummeting straight downwards. The earth rushed towards them. Blond's efforts were rewarded as the Lysander's engine caught—once, twice, then held. At the very last minute, Blond pulled back on the joystick and brought the plane out of its dive with about six feet to spare between its undercarriage and the ground.

"There it is. Two o'clock. About five hundred feet," yelled Anastasia.

"I see him."

The German pilot was surprised to see the Lysander pull out of its dive. He knew that he had hit the plane and was waiting to see the flash of fire that would confirm his kill, even if it was an unarmed plane.

His second surprise was to see the plane bank and climb steeply to his left and ahead of him, spinning wing-over-wing as it did so. Was it still out of control? It must be. Why would an unarmed plane head towards him? He watched it climb above him.

Blond, seeing the Luftwaffe fighter below him, yanked once again on the joystick to pull the Lysander into a loop. The plane dropped like a stone and levelled out only a few feet away from the surprised German pilot, who was now looking up at them with shock and amazement through his cockpit cover. Blond waved at him as he brought the Lysander down hard, directly onto the enemy plane. The wheels of the Lysander straddled the fuselage and jammed themselves into the wing structure of the German aircraft.

21

"There. You see, Anastasia. A perfect landing. Would you care to jump, now?"

Anastasia needed no second bidding. The plane-sandwich was still flying horizontally but dropping fast. As she leapt from the Lysander, she could see the German pilot struggling with the controls. He was trapped inside the cockpit. She fell away and pulled her parachute cord. What was Blond up to now?

Lieutenant Blond had climbed down the wheel frames of the Lysander and was knocking on the glass canopy of the German's cockpit. "Do you have the right time?" he shouted. "You broke my watch when you fired at us."

The pilot knew enough English to know what he was being asked and unconsciously replied, "Ja! It is two thirty."

"Danke schön," shouted Blond. "I have to meet someone. Have a good flight." He waved and then dove from the wing. He spotted Anastasia in the distance about to land, and stayed in free-fall until the very last moment to position his landing close to her. She was pulling in her parachute when Blond landed heavily beside her.

They both pulled in the silk fabric as quickly as possible and then buried the parachutes below a large tree stump. After checking over his short-barrelled Thompson machine gun, Blond pulled back the safety catch and crouched beside Anastasia.

Everything was still except for the distant whine of an engine. Then the sound of an explosion reached them, and a huge ball of flame rose in the air about two miles to the west.

"He's obviously never flown biplanes before," Blond remarked.

From a clump of trees a hundred yards away came a series of Morse Code signals from a flashlight. The Resistance had found them.

Over the next three months, Blond and Anastasia worked very closely together, each earning the other's respect and admiration. The resistance cells were now fully organized, with a flawless communication system that allowed them maximum safety and efficiency.

James received word that he was to proceed to Madrid for another assignment. N made no mention of Anastasia and Blond assumed that headquarters was satisfied with her help. Anastasia was now free to do whatever she wanted.

Their last night together was spent underneath a canopy of willows by a small stream gurgling through some very picturesque French countryside. James brought blankets, wine and an assortment of delicious cheeses and meats he had managed to obtain through members of the Resistance who had connections in the black market.

In warm breezes under a full moon, their lovemaking was something special for both of them. In wartime, such moments are particularly savoured and treasured. Heady with the wine and relaxed from their lovemaking, they fell asleep in each other's arms. When Anastasia awoke at dawn she reached out for Blond and, startled at not finding him, sat up. He had already left for Madrid.

•

There was a buzzing in Anastasia's ears and she had a nauseous feeling as her eyes slowly opened. At first the bare light bulb above her was just a blur but slowly she began to focus. The light stabbed into her eyes. She saw the evil faces of Dr. Veckoff and his associates leering over her, and suddenly remembered where she was. Dr. Veckoff was smiling.

"I admire your courage, Anastasia," he smirked, "but finally, only moments ago, you gave us the name."

"What name?" she asked, trying to collect her thoughts.

"Triple 'O' Seven."

"Triple 'O' Seven?" she repeated, genuinely puzzled.

"Yes. Triple 'O' Seven. 0007. The name that we had been trying to get out of you for the birth certificate. Congratulations, Anastasia. You are the mother of an eight-pound baby boy." Dr. Veckoff turned to the nurse. "Nurse, would you pass Anastasia her baby."

The nurse turned to a small stainless steel crib and lifted out Anastasia's baby, wrapped in army issue brown blankets. She pulled back a corner so that Anastasia could see the pink and wrinkled face of her new son. "Don't worry about him looking so ugly and scrunched-up," said the nurse as she handed Triple 'O' Seven to Anastasia. "Newborn babies are always ugly at first."

Anastasia glared at the nurse as she took the baby from her, and holding the child firmly, gave the nurse a lightning-fast chop to the throat. "Nobody calls my baby ugly," she said, looking at the infant in her arms. "Even if it is true."

Dr. Veckoff and his assistant rushed to the aid of the nurse who was holding her throat and writhing on the floor trying to get her breath.

"Good God!" exclaimed the assistant. "Why did she do that?"

"Some mothers are just overly protective," replied Dr. Veckoff. Inwardly, though, he felt as if something had snapped inside Anastasia Klause. Perhaps the effort of giving birth, together with a career in which the mind and body are under constant stress, danger and physical demand had taken her over the edge of normalcy.

Anastasia wondered how on earth her baby had been called Triple 'O' Seven. While unconscious, she must have been rambling on about her last night with Blond, and somehow they had mistakenly come up with the name Triple 'O' Seven. There was no doubt in her mind that James was the father. After all, there had been no one else.

And so it was that deep below the streets of war-torn

London, in a dingy hospital bunker, Triple 'O' Seven was born. His father: an intelligence agent with the British Government, a man licenced to kill, who knew nothing of his newborn child. His mother: a double agent, sometimes a triple agent, who had laboured in a delirium to deliver her son.

And then there was Triple 'O' Seven himself. Eight pounds of pink, wrinkled skin, gurgling with happiness and thinking of nothing except holding on to the nipple of his mother's breast, unaware that one day the fate of the entire world would rest in his hands.

Chapter Two

MOSCOW, 1983

Moscow, during the summer, is considered by some to be a rather pleasant place to live and work; but in winter, when the temperature dips below the minus-forty degree mark, everyone agrees it is a very unpleasant place indeed. When the winds from the great steppes of Siberia throw their icy hell across half a continent and into city streets, the wind chill factor sometimes takes the temperature to well below minus-eighty.

Temperature inversions force the smoke from the stacks of industrial Moscow to hover over the city, and its inhabitants, swaddled in winter clothing, breathe soot and other acrid contaminants as they struggle against winter's grip, half frozen on their way to work.

Without fail, every winter in Moscow a prolonged cold spell sets in and will not move. The very soul of the city seems to shiver, and the bleak buildings appear even more sombre as frost highlights the grime.

On just such a frigid day, a large black sedan, its windows darkened to discourage the curious, wove through the streets of Moscow and found its way to Razalav Boulevard, a narrow street running alongside the formidable eastern wall of the Kremlin. It was just after dawn and the sun, a cold white orb, hung near the horizon.

The snow made a crunching sound as the car pulled up in front of a small metal door set back into the stonework. A driver and guard stepped out and surveyed the street before opening the back doors of the sedan. The three men inside, removing themselves from the luxurious warmth of the car's interior, all gasped as they drew the icy cold air into their lungs. As one, they walked quickly to the door which had now slid open. Wrapped in furs, the three men stood in an elevator made entirely of highly polished stainless steel. A fluorescent light made them look ghostly as they plummeted down into the bowels of the earth, deep below the Kremlin.

The tallest of the three was a huge black man. Almost seven feet in height, he was as black as he could be, that is, except for his hands. They were those of a white man. An accident of birth? Mixed parents? An unusual dish soap? Who could tell, or argue the point! This enormous man could have whatever colour hands he wanted. They were pink from the wrist down to the fingertips, where carefully manicured nails scratched at the head of an old white cat tucked under his arm. The cat had been left to him by his notorious father, Blofeld.

Blofeld! The infamous leader of S.P.E.C.T.O.R who had been killed while trying to execute a plan of grand scale which would have resulted in him ruling the world. The huge black man was, in fact, the step-brother of Odd Jobb, and he owed his existence to an illicit affair between Blofeld and Mrs. Jobb, Odd Jobb's mother. He had taken the first part of his father's name and his mother's surname and was known as Bloh Jobb, adding the silent 'h' to create the impression of a single nationality (German) when in fact he gave no allegiance to any country in the world.

Bloh Jobb had inherited many traits from his father, along with almost two billion dollars. He liked to murder people as his father had. He loved pain. He loved to see people hurting and begging him for release from long slow torture. He took particular pleasure in offering them a choice of ways to die and then watching them struggle with the ultimate decision. He was fascinated by why they chose one particular method over another. He was also blessed with exceptional intelligence, like his father. His I.Q. was in excess of the genius level and over the years, his mind had been responsible for incredibly complex plans concerning the economic destruction of entire third world countries.

But above all, Bloh Jobb possessed immense strength. Every day, with speakers blaring out aerobics music, he would work out by engaging in life and death combat against unsuspecting experts in the martial arts. Hired at great expense from all over the world, these experts would innocently come to the huge private gymnasium built at Bloh Jobb's estate on a private island off the coast of Florida. As a courtesy, he would sometimes let his opponents choose their favourite record. The experts were never seen again.

In the Kremlin elevator, Bloh Jobb looked down with disgust at the two men on either side of him. They were by birth the twin sons of another respected leader of S.P.E.C.T.O.R. who had also attempted global domination. But how these two could be twins defied even the mammoth intelligence of Bloh Jobb.

Dr. Maybe was an albino, with a shock of white hair done in an outrageous punk style. The man's eyes were pink and matched the ring he wore in his left ear. Underneath the fur coat he wore a string vest, blue satin pants and black pixie-like boots. There was a slight touch of makeup around the eyes, exaggerating the already pronounced femininity of the man. He was gay in the most flamboyant way, and his penchant for young men was incredible. Bloh Jobb, knowing that he killed his lovers immediately after having sex with them, compared him to a black widow spider.

Dr. Yes was Dr. Maybe's brother. His features were decidedly Chinese and his skin had a yellowish glow that reminded Bloh Jobb of jaundice. His eyes, too, were yellow, and almost opaque. Where his brother was thin, he was fat; not obese, but fat. However, this did not mean that he could not move when he had to. On the contrary, when threatened, he was as agile as a cat. Indeed, he was a hunter. At an early age Dr. Yes had tasted human flesh, found that he liked it and had never stopped hunting for victims. Bloh Jobb didn't know how many people had ended up as gastronomic delights for this squat little person, but it was rumoured to be close to three hundred.

His cannibalism had begun during his brief membership in the Boy Scouts in England. His father insisted that he enjoy the Boy Scouts, but Dr. Yes hated all that walking through the boggy marshes of Dartmoor. Even more, he hated the Scout Master who led a particular expedition of four boy scouts and himself. The young Dr. Yes had managed to last the first two days. His feet were sore, and he was tired and hungry. Around the campfire that night, the subject of cannibalism came up as part of a discussion on survival. The Scout Master had thrown out the question to Dr. Yes: what would he do in such a situation? Not really being part of the group, Dr. Yes had just shrugged his shoulders.

The following morning, the Scout Master would not let him have a second bowl of Weetabix to appease his hunger. In a rage, Dr. Yes had grabbed an axe and killed the Scout Master and the other four scouts. For three weeks, he had lived on boy scouts, preparing them in a variety of ways. He returned home looking well nourished.

Confessing to his father, he expected to be tied on the rack and stretched for a while, as he usually was when he did something wrong, but instead his father laughed and slapped his thighs in merriment. It was the first time his father had ever given him his approval. He always remembered that as his father laughed he kept spluttering the boy scout motto, "Be Prepared", and this would send him into new peals of laughter. Pleased that he had amused his father with something he had done, he continued with his eating of human flesh. His father delighted in making jokes about his victims. When Dr. Yes ate two nuns from a convent in Oxford, his father laughed when anyone spoke of his son's eating habits. When he ate a champion wrestler, Dr. Yes had indigestion and thought he was going to throw up. His father laughed and told him to try and hold him down.

Bloh Jobb shivered involuntarily as he thought about being eaten by this man. He clutched the cat a little tighter. The elevator finally came to a stop and the stainless steel doors slid open. The threesome walked into a large room with a tremendously high ceiling. All of the walls were covered in red velvet and gold leaf. The plush, thick carpet matched the colour of the walls perfectly. A large cut-crystal chandelier hung from the ceiling and cast colour spectrums on the walls. An unreasonable number of la-z-boy reclining chairs were scattered about.

At the far end of the room, seated behind a large wooden desk, was the man they had come to see: General Mikhail Bretzky, top man of all terrorist and murder activity world wide for the hidden Soviet intelligence.

As the three approached the desk, General Bretzky rose from his chair to greet them. They moved closer to the desk and all felt a coldness in the room. The man had just risen from a chair. He had not said a word, nor made any threatening action toward them, yet they all felt the chill of fear. This was the first time any of them had met the legendary

31

General Bretzky.

The General was almost sixty years old and yet he looked no more than forty. He was tall and muscular and stood ramrod straight in his impeccable uniform. It was his eyes to which all three found themselves riveted. They were coal black and unblinking. The General was an incurable insomniac and workaholic. As he never slept, he had had his eyelids surgically removed. He had attempted to force this peculiarity onto his staff by suggesting to his superiors that all operatives have their eyelids removed in order to make them better men and women in the field. He maintained that the amount of energy consumed by the human eye blinking several thousand times a day could be better utilized. His suggestion was still under review.

One of the side effects of having his eyelids removed always pleased him very much. This was the way people he met were transfixed by his eyes. He felt like a snake toying with a hypnotized and therefore helpless animal. Exactly as these three were now.

Bloh, Yes, and Maybe shuffled uncomfortably, waiting for him to speak. He deliberately refrained from saying anything just to watch their reactions. He had spent many years at interrogations using subtle and sometimes not so subtle methods of extracting information. One method was just to look at an individual and see how long it would be before they would say something. He had the files of these three on his desk, but there was no need to refer to them. The General was blessed with a perfect photographic memory. But there was really no time to waste playing waiting games so he decided to curtail his pleasure and get on with business.

"Gentlemen, welcome to Moscow. There is no need to introduce myself as you all know who I am. However, I must first caution you that as far as all of you are concerned, this meeting will have never taken place." A buzzer rang on his desk. "Ah! Tea is served." A uniformed soldier carried in a silver tray with four very delicate china cups and a silver tea service. "I know that you would all love a refreshing cup of tea."

The statement was more of an order than a suggestion. He showed them where they were to sit. They handed their heavy fur coats to the soldier who hung them up on a nearby coat rack. The soldier then went about serving tea to the four men. As he was about to leave, the General asked the soldier to sit with the other three men and help himself to some tea. Surprised, the soldier looked questioningly at the General.

"Go ahead, have some tea and sit down. Here, you may use my cup. You have been serving me tea for almost twenty years and I think that you should finally enjoy the benefits of this delightful brew. Besides, you are a very loyal soldier and I wish to demonstrate a point to our guests."

The soldier was clearly uncomfortable as he sat down and reached for the General's small china cup.

"That's right, make yourself comfortable and enjoy your tea." The General sat at his desk and looked at the four of them sipping from the tiny cups. His rigid black eyes studied them all silently. Suddenly, he reached out and pressed a button on top of his desk. From the floor beneath the chair in which the soldier sat, a steel spike shot out of the floor with a small explosion. The five-foot spike passed through the soldier's body and out the top of his skull, killing him instantly. His military cap spun slowly on the tip of the spike. Blood began to pour from the top of his head and from his mouth. Bloh Jobb, Dr. Maybe and Dr. Yes all sat immobile. They stared at the soldier.

"I wanted to drive home a point before we begin," said the General. "I will not accept any incompetence. That man has been serving me tea faithfully for twenty years. He knows very well that I always have my tea stirred anti-clockwise and that the milk always goes in last, after the tea." As he spoke, he leaned forward and started to shout, each word accompanied by the beat of his fist on the desk. "The stupid man got the milk thing right but stirred it clockwise!"

The General gathered himself and spoke with a quieter voice. "A little more tea, perhaps?" He picked up the silver teapot and poured more tea into each of their cups. His eyes still held them in a trance. Bloh Jobb shifted uncomfortably in his chair, trying to see if there was a spike set to go off beneath him. The movement was not missed by Bretzky.

"Gentlemen, as you know, the track record of S.P.E.C.T.O.R. since the Second World War has been less than successful. And despite the fact that we have poured millions of rubles into assisting their various schemes, S.P.E.C.T.O.R. has worked against us on occasion.

"Therefore, as of now, S.P.E.C.T.O.R. is no more. A totally new organization with a budget of one billion U.S. dollars has been formed. It will operate without any official Russian aid or association. This new organization has only one aim: the total destruction of world economies, with special emphasis on the United States. You three gentlemen have been chosen to carry this out, starting immediately.

"Bloh Jobb will head up this new organization for the first year. From that point on, the leadership will be open to anyone who can take control."

The three men in front of him looked at one another. The General could sense their devious minds already working on how they might eliminate one another.

"As to what you are going to name your organization, well, that is completely up to you. You will have total control of everything that happens. You must remember, though, that failure will not be tolerated." The General walked over to the coat-rack and gave them their fur coats. They were being dismissed. "Now," said Bretzky, "as I mentioned, officially you will be on your own. However, unofficially, you will be reporting to me through my secretary." An old lady entered the room, shuffling and scuffing her feet across the floor. "Gentlemen, I would like you to meet Irma Klogg, a very trusted associate of mine. Her daughter gave her life for S.P.E.C.T.O.R. some time ago in Venice. Fortunately, her son is alive, and a top agent. You see? She dedicates her children to our mutual cause. Take note of her devotion, gentlemen."

Bretzky moved behind his desk and sat down. A smile came to his face. "Irma was the inventor of the poison-tipped blades in the shoe toes. The shoes she is wearing at this moment are deadly, so don't annoy her under any circumstances. Bloh Jobb, you will be reporting directly to her. Any unfavourable reports from Irma will result in your elimination." For effect, he pushed another button and a second steel spike shot up through the chair where Jobb had been sitting. A shudder ran through the huge man.

As they entered the elevator, Dr. Yes turned to the General and asked in a very polite voice and with a lick of his lips, what the General was going to do with the body of the soldier. Bretzky just looked at him with piercing eyes and said nothing.

The three men and Irma Klogg stepped through the little metal door, and when they arrived at street level, the guard and driver of the large black sedan were there to meet them. The car headed for a secluded airstrip where a large private jet waited with engines howling, ready to take them on the first leg of their journey to the United States.

•

Irma Klogg was sixty-nine years old and looked it. Her grey hair was swept back tightly and held in a tightly-wrapped bun. The fur coat she was wearing hung heavily on her frame. Until this morning, she had not known that she was going to the United States.

Having been a secretary for the General for many years

and an operative in the field before that, she knew that the General was under a lot of pressure to get positive results. She also knew that if the General did not deliver those results to his superiors, all their jobs, not to mention their lives, would be on the line. At her age, she was resigned to the fact that she would die soon. When the General had summoned her to his office, she instinctively knew that something was in the wind, but she was still not over her surprise at the enormity of her new responsibilities. For the first time in her life she had real power, even if it was over three very strange men.

She felt an instant dislike for the two so-called twins, but the big black man with the cat made her feel weak at the knees. It had been so long since she had felt that way. Most men were weaklings, but this man with the cat.... She smiled a little at the thought of what it would be like to have him at her beck and call.

When they entered the plane, Irma made a point of sitting next to Bloh Jobb. She left her coat around her shoulders and made herself comfortable, then smiled at Bloh Jobb, who was clearly unhappy with her choice of seat. He moved as far away as possible and placed the cat between them. The cat didn't like being used as a divider. Irma Klogg smiled inwardly and had to hold back a chuckle. If Bloh Jobb could guess what was in store for him, what would he do? She reached over to stroke the divider, and it suddenly spat and tried to scratch her with its razor sharp claws. She withdrew her hand quickly but managed to touch Bloh Jobb's muscular leg in doing so. A ripple of sexual excitement ran through her. She made up her mind that she wanted only one thing from the life remaining in her frail body: as much sex as possible with the man sitting beside her. So much sex that she hoped she would die 'the sweet death' on top of this man.

Bloh Jobb's mind was working overtime. He had one billion dollars to play with and leadership of a new organization
for one year; forever, if he played his cards right. He dismissed Dr. Yes and Dr. Maybe as little threat to himself.
When the time was right, he would get rid of them and no
one would be the wiser.

He moved further away from the old lady and pretended
to look out at the clouds. Was he imagining the meaning
behind the looks she kept giving him? God-damn it! Why did
he have to be saddled with this old crow? She reminded him
of that old thing in the *Playboy* cartoons. What was her name?
Granny. That was it. Well, he would have to get along with
her until everything was set up and then she, too, would
disappear. He hoped she was not a pervert. Pervert? Bloh
kept throwing the word "pervert" around in his head. What
a great name for his new organization! He slapped his huge
thigh and chuckled, pleased with himself. Professional
Extortion, Revolution, Violence, Espionage, Revenge and
Terrorism came into being. P.E.R.V.E.R.T.

Seated some distance away from Bloh Jobb and Irma
Klogg, Dr. Yes and Dr. Maybe were in a hushed discussion.

"I think that we will actually have to work together on
Bloh Jobb if we want control of this organization. He is too
strong and too smart for one of us to handle," said Dr. Yes.

"Yes, brother Yes. You may be right. The problem is,
how do we get rid of him and get our hands on that money?"

"We will have to bide our time and plan very carefully.
One false move and he will get rid of us both. Permanently.
We must wait until this new organization is almost running
itself, and until our plan, whatever it is, is ready. Then we
must strike." Dr. Maybe started to nervously bite his nails.

"Can I have a taste?" asked Dr. Yes.

In the room far below the Kremlin, a giant screen showing a picture of the interior of the plane was set into one of the walls. General Mikhail Bretzky reclined in one of the la-z-boy chairs with a remote-control in his hand. It was an exceptionally clear picture, considering it was being transmitted from a moving aircraft. The sound was clear and he smiled to himself as he heard the twins plotting to take control of the organization. He also noted the intent look on Bloh Jobb's face. He knew that Jobb was thinking of how to get rid of the twins.

It would be amusing to see what developed. He stabbed the remote-control at the television screen and it flicked off. After struggling unsuccessfully to bring the la-z-boy into its vertical position, Bretzky finally clambered out, stretched, and strode from the room. It was time for a workout and a massage. Perhaps some wodka.

The door shut silently behind him. The dead soldier sat alone in the room, the small teacup still in his hand.

Chapter Three

LONDON 1984

There was an intangible mood of optimism hovering over the surging tide of black bowler hats, briefcases and dark pinstriped business suits as commuters swept from all points of England to the heart of one of the world's largest cities. At seven-thirty in the morning, London seemed to inhale fresh life in the form of hustling, bustling people. It would engorge them for the day and spit them out again in the evening, and then a new wave of night people would take over the streets.

It was Monday, the first day of April. A new month with a long weekend ahead. Only four days' work and then it was Good Friday and Easter Sunday. It was also April Fool's Day and many of the people were enjoying harmless pranks.

There was no way to pin down a precise reason for the optimism. Maybe it was because the sun brought a spring warmth to the faces of the people as it peeked around the corners of the old stone buildings.

The daily rush of humanity was like blood going to a heart. It gave the city a pulse. Without this steady flow of workers, the city could not function; it would become a dead and lifeless shell.

Beneath the city, the underground trains whooshed through a maze of underground tunnels, stopping only to pour out people filled with energy and purpose. The tunnels were like arteries feeding the heart with fresh blood.

Along such famous thoroughfares as Fleet Street and Oxford Street, the bustle was even more intense as those in the newspaper and international banking fields had a head start on the day's activities. The power games and the political and economic deals were already starting in the offices and boardrooms of the larger corporate and banking institutions.

Just off Leicester Square lay the seedy area of the city. For as long as anyone could remember, Soho had been the centre for crime, prostitution, and the drug trade. In small anonymous rooms, often below street-level, sex was dispensed around the clock.

A slightly-built young man in a light grey suit closed the door to one such establishment and walked up the ten or so stone steps to Brewer Street. He looked both ways as he stood at the top of the stairs and pushed the fingers of his black leather gloves until they fit snugly over his thin delicate hands. It was a ritual he went through whenever he left the small basement room. His look almost dared the other people on the street to stare. Most people seeing him coming from such a place would know that he had just been with a prostitute, and it was as if he wanted people to know. The ends of his fingers were now almost pushing through the tips of the gloves. He pulled up the collar of his long leather jacket. It was still cold in Brewer Street. It was such a narrow street that the sun had not yet risen high enough to cast its rays onto the pavement. The young man looked about him again and sauntered off towards Oxford Street. He might have been the young assistant manager in the women's wear section of a large department store.

On the black iron railing, directly behind where the young man had stood, a small printed card was attached, strung with some thin wire. On it was printed a notice:

> School Teacher. Strong Disciplinarian. Private
> Lessons. Phone for Appointment. Suzy.

Suzy was only thirty years old, and very attractive. She had been a prostitute for almost eleven years, and her beauty had endured, even triumphed over, the rigors of a tough life. Her large saucer-like eyes made her seem much younger, especially with her hair in pony tails, as it now was.

She was cleaning up the small bedroom; the young man with the gloves had just left. It had been a long time since she'd bothered to wonder about all the sexual deviations of her johns. The young man had been coming to her regularly for almost a year and in all that time, the routine had not changed.

At six-thirty every Monday morning he would arrive carrying a large plastic bag tied with string, which he would place at the foot of the bed. Then his fantasy would begin. He would dress up in a short skirt, black nylons and garter belt, a bra, and white blouse. Suzy would then help him put on a wig with cute pony tails and apply makeup. She would dress identically so that they both looked like English schoolgirls, and would then attempt to fondle him by placing her hand under his skirt. When he resisted, Suzy would have to reprimand him and push him back on the bed. They would engage in a mock struggle, with Suzy always getting the upper hand. Act One would conclude with Suzy tying him to the bed, spread-eagled and helpless.

Suzy would make sure that her breasts rubbed against his lips. Some of the lipstick he was wearing would rub onto her blouse and this seemed to excite him. She would push her nylon clad legs against his, knowing that the feel of the nylon would also turn him on. He would continue to struggle and when close to orgasm, would start to moan and breathe heavily. It was at that moment that Suzy would back away from him completely and leave him begging for her to finish.

"You're a slut!" she would say. "You need to be taught a lesson. A lesson you won't forget. Watch me as I put my boots on." Slowly she would take off her high heels and make him lick the tips of them. If he didn't, or was slow, she would slap him with a riding crop she kept bracketted to the wall. When he felt the sting of the whip, he would tremble all over. "Stay still, you slut!" she'd command. Then Suzy would slowly pull on the thigh-high boots with the six-inch heels. He would now be whimpering and pretending not to know what was next. At this point Suzy would usually wonder to herself about his childhood.

Suzy would reach for the plastic bag and slowly, very slowly, remove the string. She would then stand on the bed straddling her helpless victim and brush the bag against the entire length of his body. "Don't move, slut!" she would command; and with that, she would empty the entire contents of the bag on top of him. In it were all the grass cuttings from the lawn of his small rented house in Croydon. He mowed the lawn every Saturday especially for this session. He stayed completely rigid on the bed and slowly disappeared from sight under a mound of grass clippings. All that Suzy could hear was a groan of sexual delight from under the pile.

Having made a few last-minute adjustments to the arrangement of grass, Suzy would go to the closet and pull out a Weedeater grass trimmer — a popular lawn care utensil. She pulled out the length of nylon cord from its spool and plugged in the electrical cord. With a whir, the nylon cord spun around. Raising the Weedeater, she would gradually start to remove the grass cuttings from his body. The stinging cord was what gave him pleasure. It was the ultimate 'whip job.' The last grass to be removed was over his throbbing groin. With a screech, he would reach orgasm.

Suzy vacuumed up the last of the grass cuttings before heading home, thinking herself lucky she had only one client who was into Weedeater sex.

She had had a busy night. A steady stream of regular customers gave her a very good income. She took a final look around the small apartment, and satisfied that all was as it should be, she left, locking the door behind her. As she went up the stairs to Brewer Street, the sun, which had worked its way higher into the clear sky, warmed her face. She walked briskly towards her apartment on Old Compton Street for a well-earned rest, her heels clicking on the sidewalk, and drew admiring glances from a few passing strangers.

Old Compton Street was more like an alley that ran off Brewer Street. If you looked upward, the walls of the buildings seemed almost to touch the sky. Suzy heard a strange noise from one of the passageways that ran between every second building. It sounded almost like a scuffle, but not really. Her curiosity got the better of her. She took a few hesitant steps into the dark passageway, and heard the noise again. It was coming from a small alcove directly to her left. She peered into the alcove, her eyes struggling to adjust to the lack of light.

Her brain had barely enough time to register pure horror at what she saw before a hand lunged at her throat, smashing the back of her head against the dank wall of the alley. She was already dying as the knife entered her stomach. Two small sparrows scratching on the cobblestones of the passageway some distance away from the alcove were suddenly covered in a fine spray of blood. Shrieking with alarm, they flew up between the narrow walls to the freedom of the skies. Away from the smell of death.

Just in that instant, the warmth of the sun was blocked by a small cloud, and all the early-morning commuters, as if orchestrated by some giant unseen hand, disappeared into their places of work, leaving the streets silent and empty.

•

"I don't give a God-damn! Good Friday or not, golf game or not. This is an emergency and I want you here within the hour. The Prime Minister is as close to panicking as I've ever seen her. I haven't seen her like this since the Falklands!" P slammed the phone down into the cradle. He was usually an unflappable sort as long as everything was going fine, or not going at all. The last thing he wanted was work. Work meant that he had to come up with results, and if he didn't get them, he could be replaced by any one of a dozen young brats in the organization who would jump at the opportunity to replace him. "Shit! Shit! Shit!" He thumped the desk and started to bite his nails, wondering what to do next. Then he savagely struck the intercom to the outer office. "Bert!"

"I've told you not to call me 'Bert'," came the reply. The voice sounded tinny through the intercom.

"Bert! You get your God-damn ass in here."

"No," came the reply.

"Bert! Don't you make me come out there and get you," P said in a menacing tone.

"Oh, P. I love it when you are so forceful. But I'm not coming in there until you comply with Government Regulation C109 dash four paragraph two, which states that all secretaries are to be addressed or summonsed by their full name whilst on duty. I hardly need to remind you of that...do I?"

P stared at the intercom box and placed his hands around it wishing that it was Bert's neck. Silently, he cursed all government rules and regulations giving equal rights to

44

minorities, sexes, and freaks. He was trapped in an intolerable position which was driving him crazy. He threw up his hands and hit the intercom again. The buttons all lit up. "All right, Mizzzzz Mummypenny," he said, emphasizing the 'Ms.' until it sounded as if an African killer bee was loose in the room. "Now get your ass in here on the double. I have a letter I want you to take down."

Bert's mother had worked with the Special Intelligence Group for almost thirty years and had made sure that her son filled her position when she left. The hours were good, the work was not that hard and the security of a government job, especially a high paying one, was easy to live with.

P, who likewise also inherited his father's job as top man at Special Intelligence, had taken an instant dislike to Bert when he noticed swellings on the chest of the boy. Bert appeared behind the typewriter the following day in a dress of frilly pink material. Bert, it turned out, was a transvestite undergoing hormone treatments.

P tried to have him fired immediately, but Bert had gone to the union and there was absolutely nothing P could do. It had been three years now since Bert Mummypenny had been his secretary, and P knew he was the laughing-stock of the entire Special Intelligence Branch. Jokes about him having an affair with his secretary were circulating daily.

Bert Mummypenny wobbled into the room on his high heels. He had never quite learned to walk properly in them, despite paying three hundred pounds cash for a modelling course. As a woman, he had abominable taste in clothes. He had a closet-full of the most nightmarish costumes and wigs imaginable. They could and did scare a lot of people at first sight. As he drew closer to P's desk, P took one look and covered his face with his hands, shaking his head. Bert was wearing a mini-skirt of brown leather adorned with sewn-on white vinyl circles, and black mesh stockings with a run on the left leg that stretched up from his shoe to the top of his thigh. He had snagged them with the heel of his right shoe while trying to get out of his car. He could not remove the heel from the stocking and had to hop grotesquely all the way from his car to the office before he could sit down and untangle himself.

He was also wearing a sheepskin vest that looked like something a Finnish goat herder would wear. The whole ensemble was captivatingly complemented by dozens of different coloured chains. On his head was something akin to a fright wig with a purple streak running down the centre from front to back. He wore long false eyelashes and makeup that completely failed to cover the dark shadow of his beard.

Bert seated himself in a chair opposite P, hiking up his skirt as he did so. P looked at him between the fingers that still covered his face. Bert, aware of P's gaze, preened himself and got ready to take dictation. He sucked suggestively on the end of his pencil, but sucked a little too hard and sent the small eraser down his throat, where it stayed. He gave a huge racking cough which dislodged the sopping wet eraser and propelled it onto the gleaming surface of P's desk, leaving a trail of spit as it rolled. It finally came to a stop inches away from the edge of the desk, and P's lap. P looked at it with disgust and horror.

"Ready, Chief," said Bert in a sultry voice, oblivious to the fact that one of his eyelashes had been dislodged and was now above his eyebrow.

"Oh, fuck!" said P, staring at the wet trail across his desk.

As soon as Bert heard the word "fuck", he brightened. He had just been given an opportunity to really needle his boss.

"That's an interesting way to start a letter, you know," said Bert, carefully jotting down the word. "Not many people really know how interesting that word is, although they may use it a hundred times a day."

He warmed up to the lecture he was about to give, noticing

with glee that P was sinking lower and lower into his high-backed, plush leather chair. "Its probable etymology was as an acronym of 'For Unlawful Carnal Knowledge' in Puritan England. It was placed on the stocks which held convicted adulterers, as an inscription for all to see. However, in recent history, the word fell into disfavour, particularly during the Victorian Era, and gave way to such euphemisms as *make love to*; *to cop, cover, lay, hump, bang* and *screw*, depending on the gentility of the speaker or of the occasion. You see, the word has been put underground, so to speak, and this has taken it out of the care of lexicographers who would have defined the limits of its meaning and usage, and the word has been left with a plethora of meanings and a confused status."

P gritted his teeth until they hurt. He was rapidly losing control of himself. Bert had a Master's Degree in English that allowed him to be very much in command of the language. He watched as Bert shifted around in his chair and got his second wind.

"For example," Bert continued, "as a part of speech, it may be used as an interjection: *Fuck, it's a warm day*; as an adverb: *It's a fucking warm day*; as an adjective: *It's a warm fucking day*; as a noun: *It's a fuck of a warm day*; as a gerund: *It's a warm day for fucking*; and as an infinitive: *It's too warm to fuck*.

"Now then, as a noun with the 'er' suffix, it can mean (Bert smiled as he saw P sink even lower): an idle person: *John is a dog fucker*; an irrelevant person: *John is a mother fucker*; or one who indulges in political sabotage: *John is a rat fucker*. Used with an adjective, it can place the entire emphasis on the modifier and none on the modified word itself: *John is an old fucker*. Of course, this is a comment on his age and not his social behaviour."

Bert saw that P was starting to go a very deep shade of red that was slowly spreading from his neck upwards. He knew he had this man, his boss who had been trying to fire him for three years, and now it was time to twist the knife. Bert cleared his throat before launching forth in his best voice.

"But it is as a verb that the word is most confusing. It may be active: *John fucked Mary*. Or passive: *John was fucked by Mary*. Its past tense denotes a spirit of reform: *I used to fuck*. Its present tense denotes a sense of defeat: *I'm fucked*; and its future tense denotes a sense of wonderment: *Well, I'll be fucked*."

Bert's grammatical lecture was having the desired effect. He was surprised that P had not yet blown his stack because the contortions on his face indicated a major eruption. Bert was determined to take P to the limit.

"Used with a first person pronoun, it conveys acceptance: *Fuck me*. With a second person pronoun, it conveys rejection: *Fuck you*. And with a third person pronoun it conveys a lack of concern: *Fuck it*. However, use it as an intransitive verb and it denotes aimlessness: *John fucks around*, or *Mary fucks about*; or incompetence: *Fred fucks up the works*." Bert, seeing that P was starting to twitch and his eyes were bulging from his face, began to speak a little faster.

"In the passive voice, it can express delightful submission: *John got fucked by Mary*; or just victimization: *John got fucked by his insurance company*.

"In the imperative mood, it can express a longing for life of leisure: *Fuck work*. Displeasure with the established order: *Fuck the system*. A desire to be left alone: *Fuck off*. A healthy attitude toward society: *Fuck everybody*. Or finally, you can use it as an interjection to express dissatisfaction with one's lot in life: *Fuck*. So you can see that despite all the confusion, its prudent and proper use can add colour and emphasis, as well as an aura of frankness, to your everyday speech or letter. And that's why I think it's a good way to start your letter."

"FUUUUUUUUUCK!" screamed P.

"Ah, I see you're dissatisfied with something. But perhaps it...." The rest of what Bert was about to say was lost as P lunged across the desk and clamped his hands around Bert's throat. Together they fell backwards from Bert's chair and onto the carpet. Bert grasped for the hands at his throat, and tried to scratch at P's eyes at the same time. Furniture flew and shattered as they rolled across the office floor. One of the table lamps fell and the bulb broke, showering sparks. P was now on top of Bert, and in between his legs, but Bert's legs were wrapped around P and held him like a vice. Bert, his strength fading fast, tried in vain to dig his high heels into P's back.

P was like a crazy man. The three years of anger and frustration at having to work with Bert, and all the ridicule he had had to put up with, was all transferred into his fingers as he squeezed Bert's throat.

"Good God!" exclaimed Inspector Truscott as he walked into the room and saw what looked like an attempt by P to rape his secretary. He rushed over to where the two of them were battling and jumped on P. "Unhand her, you swine," he yelled, dragging him away from Bert. "What on earth is going on here?"

Bert pointed at P with one hand and massaged his throat with the other. He tried to speak but no words would come out. Realizing it was futile to try anymore, he crawled slowly out of the room and back to his desk.

P stood up and attempted to straighten his tie, without success. He had never liked Truscott, either, and almost wished that he could continue the scrap with him, but he had to retain some dignity.

"Well, as you know," said P as he sat behind his desk trying desperately to calm himself, "we here at Special Intellligence always keep ourselves, in fact we pride ourselves on keeping fit...and always encourage one another to engage in...hand to hand combat, at every possible opportunity, to keep ourselves...razor sharp." It was a lame explanation, but he didn't really care if Truscott believed him or not. Truscott gave him a withering look, then came over, picked up the chair in front of P's desk, and sat down.

"I came as soon as you called," said Truscott. "What's all the flap about? It had better be serious to call me in on a holiday, I was all set to play a round of golf with the brass at the Yard."

"Don't they do anything else at Scotland Yard besides play golf?" asked P, searching through the pile of files that had managed to stay on the corner of his desk. "As it is, Special Intelligence has had to come up with the identity of that corpse they found with the prostitute in Old Compton Street."

"You have an I.D.? Is this what all the fuss is about? Well, who was it?"

"It was Professor Donald Lawrence."

Truscott rolled the name around in his mouth for a few seconds, then it hit him. "Oh, my God! He's the scientist who won the Nobel Prize for Chemistry. Donald Lawrence, recognized as one of the world's leading minds in the area of chemical warfare. What the hell was he doing in London with a prostitute?"

P shrugged. "That's why the Prime Minister is in such a flap. He was supposed to be meeting with her this week to provide details on some new work which could determine who would be the number one Global Power. Apparently, it had the nuclear and atom bomb stuff beat all to heck. It looks as if he was intercepted on his way here, and...."

"And ends up with his face and fingers eaten off in a back alley. What about the girl?"

"Unfortunate," replied P. "As far as we can tell, she came upon the killer in the act of eating Lawrence, and she herself was killed. God! I still shudder. What kind of fiend could eat the raw flesh of its victims?"

"It's hard to imagine that kind of appetite," agreed Truscott. "Christ! I wonder what this Professor Lawrence had?"

"Whatever it was, we have to find it quickly. The Prime Minister has said that we have to assign an agent immediately, the only problem is that we don't have any agents who could handle something like this. They are either all too old and in nursing homes, or they're dead. We haven't had to handle anything like this in years. The computer is checking personnel lists right now. Frankly, Truscott, we might have reached the bottom of the barrel." P stabbed at the intercome. "Mizzzz Mummypenny, has that computer printout arrived yet?"

"It's just arrived, I'll bring it in." Bert's voice had a very hoarse sound to it as it came over the speaker.

Bert walked in still holding his throat. He put an extra wiggle into his walk as he passed Truscott and placed the printout on the desk. He knew that Truscott liked him.

"Wonderful girl, that," said Truscott as he watched Bert walk out and close the door. "It's a pity we can't find more like her for the Service."

P ignored Truscott's comments and started to pore over the printout. His department had been under severe cutbacks on personnel over the last five years and agent-wise, there really wasn't much left. Those left were not available immediately as they were occupied with foreign assignments. It would be difficult to pull any of them away. At the bottom of the page, P saw the name Anastasia Klause. There followed a list of credentials, but she was living in an old folks' home in Sussex. What did catch his eye was that she had a son who had worked with her in the field for some years. Nothing major, but fully trained and available. There was something vaguely familiar about his name. P had never met the man since he had never worked for Special Intelligence directly. He really had no choice.

"Mizzzzz Mummypenny, get me Triple 'O' Seven."

Chapter Four

LOS ANGELES

Even for Los Angeles, early Easter Sunday morning, it was hot. The sun, still hidden by the hills and canyons that led down into the huge land basin that held the city, gave a purple hue to the magnificent backdrop.

Later in the day the streets would be filled with people attending churches of the more established religions. Even more would be streaming toward the beaches. But at the early hour of eight a.m., the streets were quiet.

At a small sidewalk cafe in the east end of the Hollywood area, not too far from Hayworth Street, two of the top C.I.A. agents responsible for international assignments met over croissants and small cups of piping hot, Turkish coffee. They looked a little conspicuous in their grey business suits. The few people seated around them at the small white tables were dressed in more comfortable shorts and sweatshirts. The two men spoke very quietly in short bursts, neither of them smiling.

In fact, their faces were grim and hard set. Sparrows darted around the table legs looking for crumbs, and when one of them got a little too close, one of the men lashed out at it with his foot. The sparrow had reflexes far superior to those of the man and easily avoided the kick. It hopped a few feet away and continued its search for food.

Apparently unnoticed by both men was the red Corvette with blacked-out windows that inched its way along the curb on the opposite side of the street. It finally stopped and parked, but its engine, which had a deep rumbling sound and was obviously beefed up, was left running. From behind the darkened one-way glass, two occupants observed the men.

Before too long, the older one of the two rose from the table and left for a grey Camaro parked almost directly opposite the red Corvette. The younger man looked as if he still had a little coffee to finish. He looked towards the red Corvette and nodded his head very slightly. It was the signal the occupants had been waiting for.

Joseph Martini pulled the Camaro away form the curb and headed west toward Benedict Canyon Road, where he would turn up the winding tree-covered canyon towards Mulholland Drive. Mulholland Drive ran along the ridge of the canyons for quite a distance, up into the higher hills. This was where Martini's home was, under a different name.

Martini was in his fifties, and had been with the C.I.A. for most of his life, ever since leaving the Intelligence Sector of the Marines. The purpose of his meeting at the cafe this morning had been to receive more information from Washington on the Professor Lawrence killing in London, and also to hand over the file from his last assignment, which had involved the international drug trade. He had handed over a briefcase with all the information necessary to make a clean sweep of the operation. He was pleased with the way it had gone. Steady, progressive infiltration was his trademark with the C.I.A. His work was sometimes slow, but he invariably got the assignment completed in such a thorough way that it was very difficult for any of the suspects or their batteries of sharp lawyers to dispute the evidence. Martini's work was dangerous but danger was something that gave his life a necessary spice. He never had been able to settle down.

The Camaro was approaching the junction of Benedict Canyon Road and Mulholland Drive when he noticed, some distance behind him, a red Corvette. He turned left at the junction and tried to put some distance between himself and the sports car. As the car disappeared from his rear view mirror, he loosened his tie and turned the air conditioning up. The sun beat down and the heat was already so intense that the tarmac on the road surface seemed sticky. The tires squealed even when he took easy turns. He pushed one of the buttons on the radio but quickly turned down the volume when rock music blared from the car's speakers. He punched another button and found some easy listening music. As the pleasant sounds filled the car, Martini relaxed in his seat and started to think about what he'd just been told about Professor Lawrence. He had heard of a lot of weird things in his career, but Christ! having your face and fingers eaten had to beat all. A real tasteless murder.

Even with the air conditioning on full, it was still warm in the car. He reached up to his shirt collar and pulled it open. The music started to swell with violins. He was tense, perhaps he had been working too hard. He was due for a long vacation and started to think about where he should go. Hawaii, perhaps. It was one of the best places to study birds, and this was his hobby. He had been angry at his contact for taking a kick at the sparrow, but he had kept silent. The younger man had seemed very nervous and uptight about something, so he had let it pass.... Martini had spent his last vacation in Hawaii and he'd been lucky enough to obtain permission from the State Wildlife and Preservation Department to go to Manana Island, a bird sanctuary just off the east coast of Oahu. He'd spent a week there, observing the birds, photographing them and taking notes. The weather had been perfect and he'd found himself refreshed both mentally and physically on his return.

A sudden shriek of tires and the blast of a horn accompanied by the whine of a powerful engine snapped him from his reverie. Instinctively, he slammed his foot on the accelerator. The Camaro fish-tailed and shuddered as the engine roared to full power. He glanced up at the mirror. The red Corvette was right behind him.

Adrenalin surged through his blood making his heart pound and his senses acute. His car's turbo-charger kicked in, and he jerked back into the leather seat. He pulled out his pistol from the shoulder holster and placed it on the seat beside him. He felt comforted by the feel of the heavy steel. Not bad for an old man, Martini thought.

Near the top of Mulholland Drive, the road curved dangerously. He screamed around the corner without slowing down and saw that he was starting to lose the other car. Tires squealing, he swung the car round into his driveway, hitting the fence and the rack of garbage containers as he went by. Cans flew through the air, spewing empties and paper rubbish. He brought the car to a screeching halt, leapt from the car and ran, pistol in hand, to the front door. Sweat poured off him as he scrambled with the keys to unlock the door. He cursed as he tried the wrong key, and took a quick look over his shoulder. No sign of the car, and no sound of an approaching car. Finally, he found the right key and felt relief as the door opened. The last thing he wanted was a confrontation in the open with whoever was chasing him.

After slamming the door behind him and throwing the bolt, he ran to the closed drapes. Removing the safety from his gun and holding it high, he used the weapon to move the curtains, very carefully, in order to see the driveway. Seeing nothing, he let the curtain drop and went to the other end of the large window where the view of the driveway would be better. As he looked and waited, he realized that the sweat was now pouring from him. His shirt was soaking wet and his hair damp. Wiping the sweat away from his eyes with his free hand, his heart suddenly started to pound. The long snout of the red Corvette had appeared from behind one of the hedges flanking his driveway.

The deep throaty sound of the car's engine had an ominous quality to it. He tried to see who was inside. Who the hell was it? The car came to a stop beside his own and for what seemed an eternity, he waited. The engine stopped and soon the silence played on his nerves. It seemed forever before the door on the passenger side of the Corvette opened. Again he wiped the sweat away from his eyes, and blinked.

"What the fuck?" he said to himself.

From the passenger's side a small girl, perhaps six years old and dressed in a Brownie uniform, jumped from the car. She almost fell and dropped the small doll she was carrying. She wore a brown beret over blonde hair tied in pony tails, and had a number of colourful badges sewn onto her uniform. The little girl walked around the front of the car and stood at the driver's side. As the door opened, Joe's eyes widened. Never had he seen a woman more beautiful. Flowing blonde hair cascaded over her shoulders. Long sensuous legs seemed to go on forever from beneath a short dress made only of some filmy material. Blue saucer-like eyes gave her face an angelic quality close to that of the little girl. They were obviously mother and daughter. Joe looked for weapons. The only weapons she carried were all visible to the eye. Magnificent breasts strained against the material of her dress, the nipples hard and jutting out. Joe could see she was not wearing anything under the dress. With the sun behind her, he could see right through it. Her body was silhouetted perfectly. As she reached back into the car, Joe managed to tear himself from the spell of her beauty. He was back on guard again.

The woman, whoever she was, pulled out a briefcase from the car's dark interior. The little girl had run up the steps to the front door and was now out of sight. The woman followed her daughter and rang the door bell. Joe moved softly to the door, staying to one side of it. The door bell rang once more.

"Yes, who is it?"

"Hello," came the woman's voice. "I followed you home from the restaurant. I was sitting near you and your friend. One of you left a briefcase, and I brought it back to you."

"Christ, how could he have been so stupid as to leave the fucking briefcase!" Joe muttered to himself. A wave of relief swept over him. "Just a minute," he called. Very quietly, he slid back the bolts to the door, then went across the living room and stood behind the bar, placing his gun on one of the shelves so that it would be within easy reach. He fixed himself a drink and called out, "Come on in, the door's open."

The door opened and in ran the little girl. She made a beeline for the television set and turned it on, frantically turning the channel switch until she found a station showing cartoons. She plonked herself on the floor about two feet in front of the set and seemed transfixed. It was a Roadrunner cartoon and the coyote, as usual, was using a number of Acme products and trying to get the elusive bird into the pot.

"I'm sorry," said the woman, with a voice of pure honey. She indicated her daughter with a look of exasperation. "She just loves those silly cartoons. Well, here's your briefcase." She placed it on the coffee table.

"Would you open it and just check to see if there's a red folder in there? And I'm just making a drink, would you like one?"

"No, thank you. It's a little early for me. Maybe we could

have one another time." She smiled as she struggled to open up the case.

Joe kept his hand very close to his gun. If this was a trap of some kind, this was when it would be sprung.

"There. Yes, here is the red folder." She turned the briefcase around and let Joe examine the contents. It was his briefcase, all right. He mentally cursed the young agent. There was almost a year's work in that red folder. How could he have been so stupid?

"Come on, Kitty," the woman called her daughter. "Come on, let's go."

"Oh, mommy," said the little girl, shaking her head in frustration. It looked like the coyote was just about to get the Roadrunner with an Acme bomb kit. But obediently she shrugged her little shoulders and turned off the television set. She ran to her mother and clutched at her hand.

"Thanks for bringing back the case," said Joe, hoping now that he could keep her in his house longer. It looked as if he had over-reacted, but it was better to be safe than sorry. Before he could ask them anything else, they were out the door. He followed them to the door and watched as they got into the car. The little girl waved goodbye and he did the same. The woman also gave him a friendly wave, then disappeared from view behind the blackened windows.

He closed the door and went to the edge of the curtains to watch them drive out. The car engine throbbed into life. As the car pulled away, he noticed the California licence plate. It was one of those personalized vanity plates that some people liked. From his shirt pocket, he pulled a pen and a scrap of paper. There really was no need to write it down; it was easy to remember. The orange letters on the blue plate spelled PUSSY. He wrote it down anyway, and grinned as he did so. He would check later to see who she was and where she lived. Right now, it was time for a drink.

On his way to the bar, he noticed that the little girl had left her small doll in front of the television. He picked it up and laughed. It would be a great reason to get in touch with the woman again.

Martini turned the doll upside down and looked at the red label on the bottom. *Another Acme Product* the label said. He laughed again as he recalled the coyote using an Acme product to blow up the Roadrunner. He took another step towards the bar before spine tingling terror made him freeze in his tracks. He stared at the doll with horror and lifted it up to his ear. It was ticking. Joe's last thought was the sudden realization that the woman had not been the killer. It was the little girl!

The bomb, small but very powerful, blew Joe to pieces. The windows of the house exploded outward and showered the Camaro. There was nothing left of him except some blood-stained fragments of clothing.

•

Easter Sunday in London is much the same as it is over most of the Christian world. Church bells summoned their congregations throughout the day, and at twilight, families were as families should be, together and relaxed and enjoying one another's company.

But at the offices of British Special Intelligence, all was not quiet. P was on the rampage again, convinced that he was surrounded by incompetents. He had all available staff double and redouble their efforts to locate Triple 'O' Seven. The last they had heard of him was that he had been in the casino in Monaco. He had won a lot of money and just disappeared from sight. However, with the assistance of Interpol and dozens of police forces around the world, the trail of Triple 'O' Seven was slowly uncovered. Too slowly, thought P. The intercom spluttered and Bert Mummypenny's voice, still sounding a little hoarse, came through.

"It looks as if we have him, P."

"Where?" barked P.

"New York just called and said that they are on his trail and should be able to get back to us within the hour. They are having him followed by four of New York's finest."

"Get back to them right away and tell them not to alarm him. There's no telling what he might do. Nobody knows anything about him. Use force only if it's absolutely necessary."

P sat back and smiled, pleased with himself. It hadn't really taken all that long to track him down. Two days. Not bad.

The telex in the corner of the room started to spit out messages. P got up and looked at the words as they came over the wire. It was a detailed report on the murder of a C.I.A. agent named Joseph Martini. At the bottom was a request for any information from Special Intelligence files concerning S.I. cases that this Martini may have been associated with. The only clue they had was a piece of paper with the word PUSSY printed on it. The writing was definitely Martini's and the lab had determined that it was written shortly before he was killed. P tore the paper from the telex machine, walked back to his desk, and studied the request. Why would anybody write PUSSY just before getting blown to pieces? He stabbed the intercom to Ms. Bert Mummypenny.

"I'd like you to find PUSSY for me, Mizzzz Mummypenny."

"I beg your pardon," came the indignant reply.

"PUSSY. Do I have to spell it out for you?"

There was a pause at the other end of the intercom. "What do you want it for?"

"What?" said P.

"What do you want pussy for?" answered Bert, still puzzled.

"I want to feed it into the computer and see what comes

up. If there is any PUSSY on file."

"Ah. Yes. I see," said Bert with sudden comprehension. "Right away." P looked from the intercom to the telex and back again. Aside from the strange behaviour of his secretary, things were moving well. He was pleased with himself. Something positive had been accomplished. He had time to go to the cafeteria and have something to eat. He would be back in plenty of time for the phone call coming in from New York.

It would be interesting to see this Triple 'O' Seven. He had a good feeling about this man, even though they'd never met. Yes, thought P, he was really looking forward to meeting him.

Chapter Five

NEW YORK

Triple 'O' Seven tossed a coin to a newspaper vendor and the vendor touched the peak of his cap and shuffled on to the next customer. Drizzle had been washing the streets of New York for the last three days. Triple 'O' Seven unfolded the newspaper against the rain and pretended to study it. Out of the corner of his eye, he saw the four men who had been following him try to busy themselves by looking into a store window.

He pulled up the collar of his coat and walked towards an old illegally parked 1973 Chev. Before he got into the car, he had another quick look at the four men. They were making their way towards a late-model El Cordoba.

His assumption was correct. They were definitely after him. He jumped into the car and eased it off the sidewalk. The rear view mirror showed the El Cordoba pulling away behind him.

New York, it seemed, was a city that never slept. As he drove leisurely along, Triple 'O' Seven observed the activity on the streets. Pimps, hookers, and petty criminals all scurried around, and their principal targets were the unsuspecting tourists who flooded the streets in a state of euphoria at being part of the 'Big Apple'.

A stream of yellow cabs filled the streets with noise as they honked their horns and competed for the late night theatre crowds. New York had its own character and its own smell, an unpleasant damp smell that sometimes made your nostrils slam shut. But then there were the pleasant smells, thousands of them, as the deli's, easily the best places to eat in New York, fed hundreds of thousands of people whose ethnic origins demanded those highly-spiced sausages, meats and fried vegetables.

The streets were slick with the drizzle. Head and tail lights, flashing neon, and street lamps spun a dizzying myriad of colors and turned the street into a soaking wet, Oriental rug. The city never slept: it throbbed day and night with life, creativity, violence and sex.

Triple 'O' Seven drove through the Holland Tunnel, the Hudson River moving sluggishly above him. He was heading downtown to the New York Hilton where the top two floors had been given over to a high society fund raising event. The theme of the party was Hobo and Hooker; appropriately named, as the funds were to be used to help such people on the streets of New York. The male guests were to retire to the top floor, where they could be joined by the women, to gamble at the various tables; the floor below was strictly for women only, the women had planned their own entertainment. All the men were dressed as hobos and all the women were dressed as they imagined the hookers only two blocks away would be dressed.

Triple 'O' Seven was gangly but rugged looking with a full head of dark hair. His face, with its two-day growth of beard, was chiseled. Strong planes gave a mild checkered look to his face under the fluorescent lights of the tunnel. His eyes were dark and always seemed to have a sparkle of fun in them. His lips were bordering on the sensuous and, as he grinned, he revealed strong white teeth. He was grinning to himself because he had just thought of a way to deal with the men following him.

When he emerged from the tunnel, he reached over and removed from the glove compartment his pistol and the silencer that went with it. He placed the weapon on the seat beside him and dropped the silencer into his pocket.

It was a strange sight that greeted him at the Hilton: all of the social elite of the city were arriving dressed as hobos and hookers. Cars passing by honked their horns even louder as they slowed to watch the Mercedes, Jaguars, and Rolls Royces disgorge their cargoes of scantily clad women in high heels, coloured stockings and low-cut dresses. They all had outrageous make-up on. The men looked more like clowns than hobos because, although they wore old clothing and worn-out shoes, all the articles were clean and had an artificial look that really fooled no one.

Triple 'O' Seven, in contrast, had tried to look like the genuine article. He actually looked and smelled like a hobo who had been on the rails for a long time. He drove the battered Chev up to the front entrance of the hotel and waited for valet parking. The El Cordoba had pulled up right behind him. The doorman opened the door of the Chev and his nose twitched with disdain as he held it open. Triple 'O' Seven could sense that the doorman was not exactly having a stellar evening. He fumbled around in his jacket looking for something to give to him which would make his evening just a little more bearable.

"Here you are," said Seven as the doorman held out his

hand expectantly.

"What's this?" questioned the doorman, looking at the object in his hand.

"Try it; it's good. It's a peanut butter and jam sandwich. Have a good evening." Triple 'O' Seven left the doorman wondering what to do with the dripping sandwich and saw that the four men were just piling out of their car.

As he entered the lobby of the hotel, the radio crackled in the El Cordoba. A voice came over the radio saying they were now to bring Triple 'O' Seven to Kennedy Airport immediately where a government jet was waiting to take him to England.

"Must be some special dude," commented one of the men.

"Hurry, let's get him or we might lose him in this bunch of crazies."

The four men left their car blocking the driveway, much to the annoyance of the people behind, who started to honk their horns in typical New York fashion. One of the men, the smallest of the four, flashed his I.D. card at the doorman, who still held the sandwich in his hand, and told him to leave their car where it was until they came back. Then he ran after the other three and joined them in the hotel.

The lobby of the New York Hilton was filled with people dressed in the hobo and hooker costumes. The regular guests, who were waiting in line trying to book rooms for the night, probably wondered if they were checking into the right place.

Triple 'O' Seven had made his way past the elevators and now lingered in the open bar area, which was packed to capacity. The four men came around a corner and spotted him at once.

"There he is," shouted one, and immediately gave chase. The others followed in hot pursuit, which was exactly what Triple 'O' Seven hoped for.

Pushing through the crowds, Seven made his way to the stair exit. He pushed open the door and gave the four men what he hoped was his best furtive, scared look. The four men, seeing their prey poised on the brink of escape, redoubled their efforts. One knocked over a waitress and her tray went flying as they pushed through the crowd.

In the stairwell, Triple 'O' Seven calmly waited behind the door. He pulled the pistol out from his jacket pocket and held it lightly in his hand.

The first of the four men burst through the door. Triple 'O' Seven gave him a quick blow to the back of the neck and he dropped like a stone. The other three men following directly behind tripped over their partner and fell in a mass of tangled arms and legs on the concrete stairwell floor.

"Don't make a move or you are dead," commanded Triple 'O' Seven.

"But..."

"Shut up," said Seven. His eyes were icy cold. He put the barrel of the gun directly between the eyes of the man who had tried to talk, who became instantly silent. "Drag your partner into the closet over there." The three men did as they were told. "All right, strip."

They now looked at him with fear in their eyes. What was this crazy man going to do?

"Strip!" shouted Triple 'O' Seven. "And strip him, too." He indicated the man at their feet, who seemed to be coming around. "Pass your clothes here."

In short order, all four men were down to their underwear. Triple 'O' Seven kicked the pile of clothes at his feet to one side.

"I want you to know that you made the biggest mistake of your lives by following me." Triple 'O' Seven reached into his pocket, pulled out the silencer and attached it to the gun before the horrified eyes of the frightened men. "Anyone who follows me always ends up the same way."

"Don't shoot...." stuttered one of them, his eyes bulging with fear. He was covered with sweat.

"Shut up!" hissed Triple 'O' Seven. "I hate whiners more than anything else in the world."

"Please," the man whimpered, falling to his knees.

Triple 'O' Seven raised the gun and pointed it at him. "Goodbye." He squeezed the trigger. Once, twice, three and four times the silencer made its whooshing sound, and the four men recoiled against the walls of the closet, screaming as they fell to the floor.

"You bastard!" one of the men shouted, starting to get up off the floor.

Triple 'O' Seven laughed and squeezed the trigger again. A stream from the water pistol splashed over the man's head. All four of them at once realized that they had been taken in by an incredibly realistic-looking water pistol. As one, they screamed with rage and rushed at Triple 'O' Seven. With a short exultant burst of laughter, he slammed the door on the four of them and jammed a small service trolley under the handle. Then he picked up the clothes, bounded up the stairs, and stuffed them down a laundry chute. There was a sudden crash of metal behind him; the trolley had not held! Looking down the stairwell, Triple 'O' could see the shadows of the men running up the stairs after him. Curses from all four rang through the stairwell. He had the impression that somehow these people, whoever they were, could not take a joke. Triple 'O' Seven suddenly thought of the popular expression, "Fuck 'em if they can't take a joke," and shuddered at the only alternative left to him. He turned and ran up the stairs.

The four men were in pretty good shape. They were not gaining on him but they weren't losing ground either. Triple 'O' thought fast. They probably knew about the fund raising event and had surmised from the way he was dressed that he was planning on attending the function. What's more, they expected him to head for the top floor where the gaming tables had been set up for the men. The only thing to do was get out of the stairwell at the floor below, and hope they would continue to the top floor.

On the twenty-third floor, his legs felt like lead and his heart was threatening to knock him off his feet with its ferocious hammering. Thank God this was the second-from-the-top floor. Letting the door close behind him, he entered the long hallway and ran towards the elevators. It was as he feared: when the New York Hilton had a large number of people in the hotel, the elevators inevitably proved to be woefully inadequate. A crowd of women were waiting for the elevators to take them up to the gaming tables or back down to the lobby.

Triple 'O' Seven looked to his rear. To his dismay, two of the men were running after him dressed only in their under-shorts. They must have split up, with two on this floor and two going up to the top floor. He recognized one of the men as the one he had knocked out. He didn't look too happy.

Triple 'O' hurled himself through a double swinging door which he thought might be another exit to the stairwell. Instead, he found himself in a large circular ballroom with, he estimated, at least five hundred women, who cheered wildly as he entered the room. A throng of women jostled him towards the centre of the room. Loud rock music suddenly blared out, footlights flashed and another huge scream went up from the women.

Triple 'O' Seven found himself on a small circular stage with three other men. Women sitting around the edge of the stage were frantically waving handfuls of money at them.

The other three men were surprised to see Triple 'O' but because of the loud music said nothing and began to dance. Seven started to dance, too. He had found himself in the middle of a male strip show! If he danced with the other men, there might be a chance he wouldn't be noticed by the men chasing him.

The other men on the stage with him started to take off their clothes, much to the delight of the audience. It was hot in the room and the dancers were already sweating as they teased the women sitting near the perimeter of the stage. Triple 'O' Seven followed their lead and took his clothes off, too, throwing his jacket into the audience. A woman grabbed it and squealed, excited with her prize, and a number of them waved for him to approach. Cautiously approaching the edge, Triple 'O' Seven was surprised at a woman who grabbed his trouser leg and wouldn't let go. As gracefully as possible, he tried to dance away from her, but she held fast and he only succeeded in dragging her onto the low stage. All the while, Triple 'O' Seven was desperately trying to hold up his pants, but the woman hung on like a wolverine. His pants suddenly fell down around his ankles, raising another lusty cheer from the audience.

The other two dancers were now down to their 'G' strings and were allowing the women to touch them as they teased and twirled. Some of the women tried to tempt the dancers closer with the money they were waving, and when they did come close, the women stuffed ten dollar bills beneath the tiny pieces of cloth. The room was now filled with a wild sexual energy.

Triple 'O' Seven was down on his knees, still trying to get rid of the woman who was successfully removing his pants. She stood up and waved them triumphantly around her head. Another cheer from the audience! A second woman grabbed at his shirt and literally ripped it from his back, leaving only some tattered cuffs around his wrists and the collar around his neck. He felt a hand go into his briefs and jumped back. Dollar bills flew from his underwear. The stage seemed to be getting smaller and the music louder and louder. The women were closing in. A large black woman jumped on him from behind, making him collapse to his hands and knees. She grabbed the tie which still hung around his neck with the remains of his shirt collar, and started to ride him like a horse, slapping his behind. The crowd was now in a frenzy. Another female hand made its way into his shorts. Triple 'O' Seven tried to crawl away but came to a halt when he saw in front of him two sets of definitely male legs. Both men used suspenders for their socks. Triple 'O' Seven recognized them as belonging to the men that were chasing him, and looked up to see them both shaking with anger.

"Care to dance?" Seven asked, smiling.

Just as the men were about to grab him, a huge buxom blonde and a smaller woman ran across the stage and started to pull off the shorts of the two men. Another great cheer filled the room. The two men momentarily forgot Triple 'O' Seven and tried to preserve what was left of their dignity. Triple 'O' Seven noticed that the other two men had appeared in the aisle that led to the stage and were also being attacked.

The crowd had gone completely berserk. With no sense of propriety, three women leapt onto the stage and started doing their own strip tease, and Triple 'O' suddenly found himself being throttled by a big black bra. More women jumped into the action, many of them in garish hooker costumes. Clothes flew in every direction. One of the men chasing him had lost his shorts and was frantically trying to get them back. A woman threw them up in the air. A handful of loose change was thrust into Triple 'O' Seven's shorts. He had finally rid himself of the woman on his back but now she was dragging and parading him around the floor by his tie. His face was getting very red as he began to choke. He had lost one of his shoes and one sock. Another woman was trying to get the other sock. The floor was soaked with perspiration. There must have been at least a hundred people dancing and pushing each other to the roaring pulse of the music. Many of the women were now down to their underwear and even that was starting to come off. Triple 'O' Seven was still

71

choking, and still down on his hands and knees. Three voluptuous 'ladies of the evening' were now trying to pull off his money-laden shorts.

Suddenly the music stopped and the bright overhead lights came on. In the stark light, the sexual energy seemed to evaporate in an instant and, apart from a few cheers and wild screams of some who had too much to drink, the room became relatively calm.

"Buy another drink, ladies," a woman's voice blared over the public address system, "there will be a new show in one hour."

There was another loud cheer.

"For Christ's sake, grab him and let's get out of here," shouted one of the men to his partners.

Triple 'O' Seven was still trying to catch his breath after nearly choking to death. His tie was knotted tightly around his throat and he struggled to loosen it. He looked up to see the four men coming to get him. One of them had lipstick smeared all over his body and was holding onto his boxer shorts with one hand because the elastic had broken. The others had fared no better. Scratch marks and lipstick were all over their bodies. One of them had somehow managed to acquire a black bra and didn't seem to know he was wearing it.

The four men dragged him up from the floor, one punching him in the stomach. He doubled up in pain.

"Bastard!" shouted the man who hit him. It was the same man who had begged Triple 'O' Seven not to shoot him.

"That's enough," said one of the other men, stopping another blow aimed at Triple 'O' Seven. "We have a plane to catch."

Triple 'O' was dragged out of the room and into an elevator packed with women. The five men in their undershorts were making the women nervous. It didn't help matters when Triple 'O' Seven passed wind. As everybody tried to ignore the obvious, he turned to the man holding him on his right side.

"You are a disgusting person."

Now everybody turned to look at the man, who blushed various shades of red. Thankfully, the elevator reached the lobby and they all flew for fresh air.

"Who are you guys, and where are you taking me?" Seven asked.

"Shut up!" was the only reply as the four men bundled him out to their El Cordoba.

The doorman gave a sigh of relief at their return. A long line up of people whose cars had been held up by the Cordoba were arguing with him. He didn't even seem surprised that the men were wearing next to nothing. He was just happy to see them drive away.

Triple 'O' Seven sat between two men in the back seat. The other two were in the front. While one drove, the other called headquarters. Triple 'O' Seven tried to assess his position. They were heading towards Kennedy Airport, he knew that. He knew also that he was not going to be killed, at least not yet. These men had been following him for some time. If they were killers, they would have done it long ago.

"This is car eight-one-two, come in two-nine-nine."

The radio crackled. "We read you, eight-one-two."

"We have him and are heading for Kennedy Airport. E.T.A. five minutes. Contact pilot and advise."

"Will do. Ten-four."

The man in the front seat hung up the radio phone. Triple 'O' Seven had been correct. They were taking him to the airport. But why?

At Kennedy Airport, crowds of passengers stopped to stare at the strange sight of four undressed men covered with scratches and lipstick forcibly escorting another man with dollar bills and change falling out of his jockey shorts.

When the men reached security baggage check, they were halted by a young man in a guard's uniform. He looked new to the job and was taking his duties far too seriously.

"You guys got any luggage with you?" he asked.

The four men looked at him incredulously. "Do you see us carrying any luggage?" one of them replied sarcastically.

"I'm sorry, sir, but I'm afraid you look suspicious to me." The young man blocked their path to the metal detector.

"Suspicious. Ha! Suspicious. Did you know that we happen to be an elite division of the New York Police Department?"

"Oh, yeah!" smirked the young man. "And who's this? One of your finest lady cops?" He pointed with his metal detector at the one wearing the bra.

Realizing for the first time what he was wearing, the man ripped the garment from him and threw it down onto the ground. Another security man came running towards them. He spoke to the young guard and then took control of the situation.

"It's okay, gentlemen, you are cleared right through." He waved them forward.

As Triple 'O' Seven went through the metal detector, the alarm sounded. His jockey shorts were still bulging with loose change, which he tried to get rid of by walking strangely. He wondered what was going on. Why would four New York City cops be taking him to the airport at this time of night?

He was shunted towards gate fifty-four and unceremoniously dumped into the passenger compartment of a jumbo jet. It seemed very large and very empty. The door hissed shut behind him and immediately the plane started to move.

He went to one of the seats, sat down, and looked out the window. There was still a drizzle falling and the runways reflected all of the lights. The plane passed two or three other aircraft that were waiting for clearance from the tower.

Obviously, whoever had control over the plane had some pull; jumping the line-up for take-off was never allowed.

Soon the plane was gathering speed and with a sudden lurch, it was in the air. The plane made a steep climb, pressing Triple 'O' Seven back into his seat. The aircraft then dipped a wing allowing him to see the incredible spectacle of New York at night. It doesn't matter how many times you fly into or out of New York, the effect is always spectacular. A brilliant array of lights stretched as far as the eye could see.

When the plane levelled out at thirty-five thousand feet, a voice filled the cabin.

"This is Captain Ed Carter speaking. Welcome aboard flight Zero Zero Zero Seven, bound for London, England. Mr. Seven, would you please come to the upstairs cabin?"

Triple 'O' undid his seatbelt and walked forward into the first class cabin. He was still a little suspicious. Slowly, he climbed up the spiral staircase. A sudden noise made him hesitate, but only for a second. It was another quarter falling out of his shorts and tumbling down the stairs.

"Do come in, Triple 'O' Seven." The invitation was extended by a remarkably beautiful woman holding a glass of champagne and standing at the top of the staircase.

He accepted the offered glass from the woman and stepped into the cabin, which was decorated like the swankiest bedroom he could have imagined.

"I'm Candy," said the girl who handed him the champagne. She took his arm and led him to where two equally attractive women were creating bubbles in a sunken tub. "This is Sugar." She indicated a vivacious (Triple 'O' Seven guessed Polynesian) girl who smiled with such pearly white teeth. "And this is Honey." He smiled back at the beautiful blonde who was now turning her attention to fluffing the pillows on a circular bed.

"Thank God I have a sweet tooth," said Triple 'O' Seven, raising his glass to the three women.

"We are here to satisfy your every need," said Candy, trying to unknot the tie around his neck.

The cabin was sumptuously decorated with deep pile carpets in a peach colour that, under the soft lighting, gave the room a luxurious warmth. The bubbles in the sunken tub looked very inviting. After his exhausting session with five hundred screaming women, Triple 'O' Seven looked forward to relaxing in the hot water. The trip to England would take approximately eight hours. Lots of time. He gave himself over to their care.

"Here's a ten!" exclaimed Candy as she eased Triple 'O' Seven's briefs down over his hips. "Wow!" She seemed genuinely surprised.

"Well, it's not quite a ten," said Triple 'O', pleased that his physical attributes were causing such a stir. He was trying to remove the tie from around his head.

"Yes, it is, look girls," said Candy.

He found himself becoming a little embarrassed. He started to speak but Candy spoke first.

"Look, a ten dollar bill." She waved the money which had dropped out of his briefs. "And look, here's a two."

"Just how much money is in there?" said Triple 'O', finally getting his tie off.

"Well, the ten dollar bill was the last of the money. The two I was referring to was your, er..."

A surprised look appeared on the face of Triple 'O' Seven.

"But I was only joking," Candy finished. She laughed and the other girls laughed with her. They all ran over and led him to the tub.

"Let's see just how sweet your sweet tooth really is," said Sugar.

Chapter Six

HAWAII

Molokai, one of the smaller of the Hawaiian chain of islands in the Pacific, is known to most people as 'the friendly isle'.

Molokai has a somewhat sleepy quality to it. The fifth largest of the islands, its population is small. Molokai has perhaps best been known for its leper colony, established there by a Catholic priest named Father Damien, who devoted his life to easing the terrible suffering of the disease's unfortunate victims.

The leper colony still exists but, because of medical breakthroughs in the treatment of leprosy, the members of the colony have slowly diminished in number. Consequently, the colony moved from the old site founded by Father Damien and is now located in a remote village near the Halawa Valley, a lush tropical paradise of incredible beauty.

It was the kind of evening which made a person glad to be alive. A shower had erupted over the island about an hour before sunset, imparting a magical quality to the rich blanket of brilliantly coloured flowers and plants: the air was now suddenly moist and heady with the scent of the tropical flora. The rain ended as quickly as it began, leaving the sky clear and ready for another of nature's spectacular displays. The sky became a chameleon. Every thirty seconds or so, as the sun made its way down to the ocean horizon, the sky took on a different hue of brilliant colour. Even the most skilled painter could not hope to duplicate the shimmering greens, golds, purples, and reds which nature now unfolded.

Above the entrance to Sandy's Bar and Grill was a huge, carved wooden replica of the Hawaiian coat of arms. Kamehameda, an old king and warlord of the Islands who had died in the early 1800s, was pictured on one side of the coat of arms. On the other side was the picture of a Goddess holding a partly unfurled flag; and at the bottom of the flag was a Phoenix, taro leaves, banana leaves and some ferns. As the sun dropped, the shadows lengthened across the carving, giving it a sinister quality. If you let your imagination run wild, you would swear that the evil face of Kamehameda was watching, and laughing.

Sandy's Bar and Grill was located on the eastern-most tip of the Island. It was really no more than a large thatched hut with blinds that could be raised or lowered to allow a view of the sunset. In fact, the view from the bar was its main asset.

Sandy, now in his fifties, had bought the bar with his wife almost nine years ago. She had died a year ago and the bar was not kept as clean as when his wife had been helping him. The business had also suffered, customers slowly but surely drifting away to other bars. Sandy was not all that worried. He made enough to pay the bills and keep the bar stocked, but he was gradually losing interest in the business and becoming more and more engrossed in his hobby: bird watching. In fact, bird watching was consuming him. Pictures of birds hung on the walls of the bar and stuffed birds with glassy eyes hung from every nook and cranny in Sandy's Bar and Grill.

Sandy was keeping himself as busy as he could with a glass and a cloth rag. He always did this when he felt uncomfortable or nervous. The only customer in the bar was a man who had been sitting on the same stool, drinking, since noon. The man was close to passing out but incredibly, still had the ability to ask for yet another beer, and another dish of nacho chips. Sandy couldn't believe how many nachos this guy could eat.

That was the problem with owning a bar. For the most part everything went smoothly, but then some customer, and not always men, would go overboard and either fall asleep or turn violent. Sandy thought that this man had the potential to turn violent. He just looked the type.

The customer picked up his beer glass and drained the liquid in one swallow.

"Give me another, and fill up this dish," he said, pushing both the glass and the empty chip dish towards Sandy.

Sandy did not say anything as he gave the man another beer. With a bit of luck, the man would drink so much that he would pass out and not cause any damage. He slid a new supply of nacho chips along the bar. The man grunted and tossed a dollar bill down. Sandy had just picked up his glass and cloth and started to clean it again when he heard a noise from outside like the slamming of a car door. With a sigh of relief that someone else had arrived, someone who could help him if the drunk became obnoxious, Sandy walked from behind the bar to the front door to see who was there.

About one hundred yards away from Sandy, on the narrow and still-wet road, a car was pulling away. With a puff of smoke from the exhaust, it rounded a corner and disappeared from view, leaving a solitary figure standing by the side of the road. Sandy could not make him out.

In the last few minutes of daylight, it was difficult to see.

The man turned and started towards the bar with a shuffling gait. The surf crashed against the sand, distracting Sandy for a moment. He looked towards the beach and the sky suddenly turned dark as the last rays of the sun disappeared below the horizon.

Sandy went back into the bar and fished into his pocket for a quarter to put in the juke box. Soon, the cheerful sounds of Hawaiian steel guitars filled the room. Sandy looked out of the window again. Usually there was red in the sky for a while after sunset, but tonight the sky was black. A gust of wind passed through the windows, sending a chill through every part of Sandy's body. A spectacular bolt of lightning made him jump, followed by a loud crack of thunder.

As the wind quickly picked up force, the rains came with a vengeance. Sandy dropped the glass he was holding and it shattered on the floor.

Startled, he ran to the windows and lowered the blinds. The wind was blowing his stuffed bird collection about and damaging it. A bright flash of lightning followed immediately by a crack of thunder made Sandy clutch his ears. The lightning must have struck within yards of the bar. Lights went out and the juke box wailed as the record ground to a halt. A large stuffed black bird fell from the roof. He screamed as the feathers brushed his face, grabbed it, and threw it across the floor. He didn't care anymore; he felt panicky for some reason. It felt like someone was gripping his spine with a pair of pincers.

The wind took hold of the front door and blew it open and shut several times in succession. It sounded like it was ready to fly from its hinges. Sandy grabbed a lantern from the far end of the bar and pulled a lighter from his pocket. Goddamn it! Why was he shaking so much? He lit the lantern and adjusted the wick. The door blew open and shut again with a deafening slam. Sandy moved as fast as he could towards the door; he must throw the latch. Just as he grabbed the handle of the door, another bolt of lightning followed by a violent crack of thunder made the whole bar shake and rattle. Sandy was almost knocked from his feet. Regaining his balance, he reached again for the handle and tried to close the door. It wouldn't budge. Another chill, like a shockwave, sent shivers up and down his spine. He pushed harder but the door seemed to have a life of its own and pushed against him. Sandy put his shoulder to the door, to no avail.

The scream that suddenly came from Sandy's mouth expressed pure terror. As he pushed against the door a wet hand, festering with blisters and oozing blood, closed around the hand of Sandy and pushed open the door. The hideous hand was followed by a face covered with the same blisters. The light from the lantern made the face look even more terrible. Where once there had been a nose, there was now a black hole. Where one eye had been, there was just an ugly socket. The mouth was disfigured and pulled to one side.

Sandy fell back from the door, still screaming. The man followed and grabbed him from behind, placing that ugly hand over his mouth.

"Shut up!" commanded the man. Still holding onto Sandy, he kicked the door shut and dragged him backwards. The customer at the bar turned around in a drunken stupor to see what the fuss was about. He needed another beer.

Sandy was old and soon stopped struggling. Suffocated, he dropped lifelessly to the floor. The man ripped the lantern from Sandy's grasp and, ignoring the harmless drunk, made his way to the shelves of bottles.

"Gimme another beer," the drunk demanded.

Surprised by the request, the assassin turned and poured him another one, providing the drunk with a fresh ashtray for good measure.

"Thanks, Mac," said the customer, throwing another dollar bill onto the counter. "Hey, what happened to the other guy?"

"He just finished his last shift," replied the man, a hint of a smile on his face. He poured himself a large glass of whiskey and downed it in one gulp. The liquid stung as it made its way down the man's gullet, and he grimaced, making his face look even more terrible.

"Hey, Mac. You'd better take it easy on the hard stuff. That can ruin a guy. Look what it's doing to your complexion." The drunk took another sip of beer. "This is what you *should* be drinking. Ah! What the hell. Drink what you like…. Hey, bartender. You know why I'm getting drunk? I just got divorced. My wife had the filthiest habits, you know. Filthy. You know, sometimes I'd come home from a party pissed to the gills and need to take a leak in the sink. And y'know, there would still be dirty dishes in there. Can you believe that? God, she had filthy habits." The drunk swallowed down the last of his beer. "Hey, Frank, let me buy you another drink."

"My name isn't Frank."

"What is it then, Frank?"

"Leopold."

"Leopold! What the hell kind of name is that?" The drunk laughed and took the beer that Leopold held out to him. He raised his glass in a salute and Leopold did the same.

"Good health," the customer toasted.

"And long life," added Leopold. There was a reflective pause.

"I'm known as Leopold the Leper," said Leopold, pushing his grotesque face closer to the drunk to drive home his words.

"Hey, there Leo," said the drunk, raising his glass. "Hey, buddy, you should see someone about that acne. That looks pretty bad. If you want to stand a chance with the girls, you should put some kind of cream or something on your face. Hey, and what happened to your nose? No, don't tell me, you picked it when you were young, right? Well, to each his own. I was told that my pecker would drop off if I kept playing with it. You should always listen to your mother, big buddy. Hey, give me one more beer, then I gotta go.''

Leopold gave him another beer and poured another large shot of whiskey for himself. The bottle was now empty and he threw it onto the floor.

"Hey, Leo," said the drunk, his words now very slurred. "What line of work you in?''

"I'm a killer,'' answered Leopold.

"That's kind of a dead end job.'' The drunk laughed and slapped the top of the bar. Leopold just looked at him. "And how's business?''

"Pretty good, actually.''

"I never believe anyone who says 'actually','' said the drunk.

"It's true." There was an edge to his voice.

"Oh, yeah?" teased the drunk. "I don't believe you.''

"Well, I just killed him.'' Leopold pointed at Sandy, who still lay on the floor.

The drunk turned his head with quite an effort to look at Sandy. "Well, how'd you do that?''

"Suffocated him and broke his neck at the same time," said Leopold, a touch of pride now in his voice.

"Hey! That's pretty clever. Killed him twice, huh?" The drunk leaned forward and whispered, a finger across his lips, "Who ya gonna kill next?''

"Me,'' replied Leopold.

"Hey, big buddy, why you gonna do that?''

"I'm on a suicide mission.'' Leopold looked for another bottle and found some vodka. He filled his glass and took a large swallow.

"When you gonna do it?" asked the drunk.

"When I finish this drink.'' Leopold raised his glass once again.

"You don't mean right here, do you?"

"Yes."

"Hey, fantastic. Y'know, this little bar has great entertainment. Y'know?" His words were now very slurred and interspersed with hiccups and laughter. "How you gonna do it?"

Leopold pulled aside his coat and revealed five or six grenades hanging from the belt of his grimy dungarees. He pulled one out. "With this."

"A miniature pineapple." The drunk burst out laughing and slapped the bar in amusement. Leopold also laughed, but was so drunk he was having trouble pulling out the pin.

"Hey, big buddy, let me do that." Leopold was having difficulty holding himself up behind the bar, he was laughing so hysterically. He passed the grenade to the drunk.

"Hey, big buddy; Leo, Frank, or whatever your name is, we gotta do this again sometime. I haven't had a blast like this for quite a while." He pulled the pin and handed the grenade back to Leopold.

The crack of thunder outside was loud, but not as loud as the explosion that destroyed Sandy's Bar and Grill. A huge ball of fire erupted as the other grenades attached to Leopold's belt went off in quick succession. Within seconds, there was only a blazing inferno and the heavy rains lashed down but did nothing to stop the flames.

The car that had deposited Leopold on the roadside a short time before nosed forward silently to inspect the damage. Irma Klogg peered through the windshield. Her lips compressed into a thin smile. The mission had been simpler than she had imagined. It had not taken much to convince Leopold that his family would be well taken care of if he killed Sandy. Now the only possible link to P.E.R.V.E.R.T. had been eliminated. Bloh Jobb would be pleased. It was almost time to make him pay for all the help she'd given him.

She turned the car around and drove back the way she had come. .

•

The telex in P's office chattered into action as the news about the explosion in Hawaii and the deaths of the three people was transmitted.

P, who had been sleeping head-down on his desk, jumped to the machine. When it stopped, he tore the paper from the roll and studied it. P looked very tired and haggard. He had not slept very much at all. The Prime Minister had called three times asking for progress reports. He had received word from New York that Triple 'O' Seven was en route and due shortly. He had ordered that all files on Professor Lawrence be pulled from Interpol and other police agencies. Apparently, Lawrence had been working on a number of top secret projects, any one of which could spell disaster if the information fell into the wrong hands. And what was worse, although P knew *of* the projects, he could not get any specifics. Both Washington and the Defence Department in London were being extraordinarily tight-lipped.

He took another swig of his cold tea. It tasted terrible. Making a face, he pushed it away. His brow creased as he lapsed into thought. The only clue he had was that the C.I.A. agent and this man, what was his name?—he grabbed the telex sheet again—Sandy, had both been fanatical bird watchers. What was the connection? There had to be something.

He picked up a pencil and started doodling on his desk pad. He drew a bird and then made a string of dots representing bird droppings which exploded at the bottom of the pad. He made a small exploding sound as they reached their target. P's musing was interrupted by the buzz of the intercom. It was Bert Mummypenny.

"P, Triple 'O' Seven has landed at Heathrow Airport."
Bert sounded unusually animated. The office had gone to a
lot of fuss to get this man here so quickly and Bert was
anxious to see what all the excitement was about.

Chapter Seven

LONDON

Triple 'O' Seven was very impressed with the service the three girls had given him. They had done everything to make his trip as enjoyable as possible. He felt exhausted and refreshed at the same time. He did not know how, but they had provided him with an impeccable looking dark suit that fit perfectly. The suit was complemented by a blue striped shirt with a white button-down collar made of very expensive silk, a matching silk designer tie, and Italian leather shoes. Whoever he was going to see seemed to know everything about him. To complete the outfit, he was given a furled umbrella and a black felt hat, something like a bowler, but not quite. He banged the top to give it a crease, for a more rakish look.

The three girls waved goodbye to him as he left the plane and stepped into the grey Rolls Royce waiting for him on the runway. It seemed there was no such thing as Customs on this trip, and the car was soon speeding along the rain-soaked streets towards the heart of London.

Triple 'O' Seven relaxed in the back of the car and gave a lot of thought to what had happened in the last twelve hours. One thing for sure was that someone wanted to meet him badly, but he had no idea why. So far the trip had been, for the most part, enjoyable. Candy, Honey and Sugar had been delightful. He wished the plane had never landed. With a bit of luck, he would enjoy a return trip.

Triple 'O' looked out of the rain-streaked windows at the grimy exteriors of the row housing at Croydon. He had been in London many times, and this part of the city never failed to depress him. Soon he was in the centre of the city. The traffic was fairly heavy with the rush hour and everyone trying to get to work.

The Rolls was approaching a moderately tall nondescript stone building in Picadilly Circus. This was the building that housed the Special Intelligence Department of the English government. On the ground floor, a tobacconist and newspaper shop doubled as the entrance to the Department. In front of the small shop, a blind man with a seeing eye dog held out a cup to pedestrians as they passed by. He wore an old raincoat and matching old hat. His large dark glasses hid a goodly portion of his face and he had several days' growth of beard and looked very unkempt.

As the Rolls pulled up outside, the blind man looked both ways along the street. His mission was simple. Kill Triple 'O' Seven. A stiletto knife slipped down into his hand, which was covered by the long sleeve of his raincoat.

The razor-sharp dagger was held lightly, the way a true professional killer is trained to hold a knife, very much like a fencer holds his foil. It allows for dexterity of movement and a quick, accurate attack. He had only one chance at this man, and he must not fail.

The dog watched with baleful eyes as Triple 'O' Seven got

out of the Rolls. It scratched itself as Triple 'O' neared the door of the shop that the driver had directed him to go through. Triple 'O' Seven was digging into his pocket. "Here, I have something for you," he said to the blind man. The blind man was taken completely by surprise as Triple 'O' Seven whirled around and launched a high kick to the man's head. His foot landed with a sickening thud, rocked the man off his feet and sent him through the plate glass window of the tobacconist shop. As the man lay sprawled over the counter amongst a scattered array of girlie magazines, Triple 'O' Seven pushed the point of his umbrella against the man's throat. The man, already gasping for air, felt the point of the umbrella push against his Adam's apple and winced in pain.

"Make one bad move and I'll push this right through your throat. Now, if you will kindly drop the knife?"

The man slowly let the weapon slip from his fingers. Triple 'O' Seven picked up the weapon and held it up. "Hmmm. Sheffield Steel. Made in England. This particular kind of knife is select government issue. You must be working with British Intelligence. Am I correct?"

The man nodded.

"Well, next time you pull this little stunt, remember that a blind man's dog has a harness and not a leash. I don't appreciate being set up like this. The last time somebody did this to me, he ended up in hospital. Would you like to know what for?" Without waiting for a reply, Triple 'O' Seven let out a primal scream and brought the knife down between the man's legs. The man screamed. "An appendix operation," said Triple 'O' Seven, answering his own question. He pulled back from the man who looked with horror at the knife between his legs. It had narrowly missed his genitals and was stuck deep in the countertop. He fainted.

A small crowd had gathered to see what was going on.

"It's all right, everyone," announced Triple 'O'. "The

poor man fell through the window. He's okay.''

The crowd dispersed and Triple 'O' Seven walked into the shop. The manager of the shop smiled and pointed to the back of the shop, which seemed to get narrower and narrower. The wall suddenly pulled back silently and Triple 'O' Seven walked into an elevator.

In the small anteroom outside P's office, Bert Mummypenny watched a small light flashing on his desk. Triple 'O' Seven was on his way up. Bert quickly buzzed P and was now smearing another coat of lipstick onto his mouth. He was just adding a touch of rouge to his cheeks when Triple 'O' Seven walked into the office.

''Wow! What a gorgeous hunk. Hi! I'm Bert Mummypenny.'' Bert stood up and wobbled on his high heels towards him. He held out a limp hand and gazed into Triple 'O' Seven's eyes. ''I think I'm in love,'' whispered Bert.

''With whom?'' Triple 'O' whispered back.

''Oh, you're such a tease,'' said Bert. He tossed his head and wobbled back to his desk. ''Take me,'' he said, laying back over his desk and scattering the stacks of neatly piled papers. ''Take me here and now. Oh! God!''

Triple 'O' Seven looked on in amazement as Bert Mummypenny, as if in some kind of trance, started to gyrate on top of the desk. The buzzer to the intercom snapped Bert out of his reverie. He stood up and wobbled back behind the desk, straightening out his skirt and smiling coyly at Triple 'O' Seven. ''You animal, you.''

''Send in Triple 'O' Seven,'' a voice barked from the intercom.

''P will see you now,'' said Bert, a dreamy look in his eyes. ''You can leave your umbrella and hat on the stand.''

Triple 'O' Seven threw both his hat and umbrella at the hat stand. Unfortunately, he missed and both hat and umbrella flew out the open window.

Nine floors below, the umbrella, travelling at two hundred

and sixty feet per second, pierced the back of a pedestrian, felling him instantly. The hat floated gently through the air and landed in an open sports car driven by an elderly English gentleman who was so startled he spun the steering wheel causing a major automobile pile-up all around Picadilly Circus.

Unaware of all the damage his simple act of throwing the hat and umbrella out the window had caused, Triple 'O' Seven went in to meet P, the man who had gone to such extraordinary lengths to see him.

P rose from behind his desk to greet his prize. Both men shook hands and P appraised the man standing in front of him.

"I hope you didn't mind the little test with the blind man. I gave him orders to kill you but you seemed to handle it very well. I'll get straight to the point, Triple 'O' Seven. We have a problem, we think a major problem, and we need your help."

"Who are you?" asked Triple 'O' Seven.

"We are Special Intelligence for the English Government. We answer to no other than the Queen and the Prime Minister. This department has been in existence for many, many years. I don't know if you're aware of this, but your mother, Anastasia Klause, worked for us during the Second World War. You've been on our files almost since the day you were born. We know that you are a fully trained operative who has never really worked on anything major, to this point. All of our other operatives are engaged in very sensitive assignments. To pull them out now would be catastrophic, security-wise. This emergency hit us unexpectedly and we had to find someone fast. Our computer told us we should try you."

"But I haven't been in the field for ten years or so, and even when I was, I was just a courier. I don't think I'm your man. I never realized that I'd be on a computer file somewhere. I really think that you should find someone else."

Triple 'O' Seven rose from his chair to leave.

"Of course, we don't expect you to do this for nothing," said P.

"You cannot buy me, P. I'm sorry, but you will have to find someone else." He made for the door.

"The pay is really quite attractive. One hundred thousand pounds now, and the same amount when the job is finished."

Triple 'O' Seven stopped in mid-stride, and whirled around. "That is the most disgusting use of authority that I have ever witnessed. You kidnap me at gunpoint using thugs from the New York City Police Department, have me shipped over here, and then have someone waiting to kill me as a test. *Then* you try and buy me with two hundred thousand pounds." Triple 'O' Seven paused. "Did you say two hundred *thousand* pounds?"

"Yes."

"Is that cash?"

"Yes."

"When do I start?" Triple 'O' Seven returned to his chair.

"What the hell is going on outside?" said P suddenly, walking to the windows. He peered out and down to where Picadilly Circus had transformed itself into a disaster zone. Ambulances were everywhere, as were the police. People were being carried on stretchers and cars were piled up on top of one another. Triple 'O' Seven joined P at the window.

"Looks like some crazy driver has caused an accident," observed Triple 'O' Seven.

P pulled down the window in an attempt to shut out some of the noise from the street. His action did little to lessen it. "God-damn it, if I don't have enough problems without having to put up with that infernal noise. If I could lay my hands on the idiot who caused that accident, I'd have him put away just like that." P snapped his fingers.

"Now, where were we? So, you'll take the assignment?"

"Yes."

"Good. Let me say that you have already been cleared by security, and as an agent working with this department, you have to answer to no one except me. You have autonomous power to make any decision you see fit and you are also licenced to kill."

"I'm what?'

"I said that you have a licence to kill."

"Kill what?"

"People, of course."

"Listen," said Triple 'O' Seven, "I have been involved in all kinds of scraps but I have never killed anyone."

"We know that, but in this assignment, you will either have to kill a few people or they will, I am sure, kill you. Without hesitation."

"But I don't know if I can kill anyone. I mean, it's kind of drastic, isn't it?"

"I suppose it is." P pondered this for a few seconds, then dismissed the problem with a wave of his hand and punched a button on the intercom.

"Yes, U here."

"U? It's P here. Listen, I'm going to bring down Triple 'O' Seven in a minute and I want you to mix something up for him so that he doesn't have an upset tummy when he kills someone. Can you do it?'

"Of course, P."

"Thank you, U."

"Am I the only one with a normal name around here?" asked Triple 'O' Seven.

"Oh, don't be fazed by all these code names. It's government regulations. U is quite a character. He's responsible for all the gadgets we develop for use by agents in the field." P pulled out a cigarette from a silver box on his desk. He offered one to Triple 'O' Seven and they both smoked as P briefed Triple 'O' Seven on what the assignment was. In clipped tones, P began to relate the details of the four murders, begining with the gruesome death of Professor Lawrence. Triple 'O' listened quietly.

Finally, P stubbed out his cigarette. "And so, it is imperative that you find out what is going on and who's behind it all. If the deaths of the C.I.A. Agent and the owner of Sandy's Bar and Grill, and also the deaths of the prostitute and Professor D. Lawrence, are connected, then it escapes me. The only tie-in is that the C.I.A. agent and the owner of the bar in Hawaii were fanatical bird watchers. What that could lead to or mean, I have absolutely no idea." The buzzer on the intercom broke into his conversation. It was Bert Mummypenny.

"P, I have just found out about PUSSY."

"What!" exclaimed Triple 'O' Seven.

"Where is it now?" P sounded excited.

"It's on my desk, it just came." Bert sounded excited, too.

"What on earth...?" said Triple 'O' Seven.

"Bring it right in, I want to have a close look at it and I'm sure Triple 'O' Seven would, too. Wouldn't you?"

"What?" said Triple 'O' Seven again. He was still more than a little confused.

"Look at PUSSY. Of course you would. It's what we've all been waiting for."

P swept a pile of papers from the top of his desk. He was clearly excited.

Triple 'O' looked at the expanse of the desk. "Well, just how big is this 'pussy' that we are going to look at?"

Bert wobbled in as best he could on his high heels. His face was flushed with excitement. Triple 'O' Seven stood up with some apprehension and looked toward the door.

"I knew you would want to see it as soon as it came," said Bert as he made his way to the desk smiling at Triple 'O'

Seven and almost swooning. He shook his head with an exaggerated swirl which he thought was quite sexy, but this only dislodged his wig so that it concealed most of his face.

"Put it on the desk," P said impatiently.

Bert Mummypenny put down the file and sauntered out of the office. Triple 'O' Seven watched him leave, visibly relieved.

"I forgot to tell you, Triple 'O' Seven, that before the C.I.A. agent got blown to pieces, he wrote the word 'PUSSY' on a slip of paper. We fed PUSSY into the computer on the off chance that something might come up. Well, it was a hunch that paid off. Look." He turned the file around so that Triple 'O' Seven could see. P was very pleased with himself.

Triple 'O' suddenly realized what was going on. The computer had traced the word PUSSY to a California licence plate that belonged to a gorgeous blonde whose name was Pussy Love. An address was given, in Beverly Hills. The photograph of the woman was breath-taking. Very little was known about her except that she had a small seven-year-old daughter. Triple 'O' Seven also noted that a speeding ticket had been issued to her very close to the place where the agent had been blown up. He looked at a copy of the ticket and noted the time. It was only about ten minutes before the agent had been killed. She had been placed in the area and the coincidence was just too much to ignore. She had to be responsible.

"You will have to track this Pussy down," said P. "But be careful, she may be responsible for all the other deaths."

"Well, I hope this...Pussy is not the death of me," said Triple 'O' Seven to himself as he looked at the photograph.

"Well, let's go and see U," said P.

"Me?" said Triple 'O' Seven.

"No, U," said P, getting up from his chair.

"Me?" said Triple 'O' Seven again, puzzled.

P looked at him and shook his head. "Come with me." He led the way down a flight of stairs and through very busy offices. The building was like a maze. They eventually found their way to another elevator which took them to a huge laboratory where technicians worked with microscopes and played with retorts and Bunsen burners. They made their way to the back where a door barred their way. A sign said Special Weapons Section. P passed his hand over an electronic palm-print reader and the door opened.

The room was very bright and housed long benches filled with electronic gadgetry and weapons. There were hundreds of guns of different sizes. Motorbikes, cars, and what looked like a flying saucer in the far corner. P spotted U at the back of the room and led the way towards him.

They were halfway there when a fierce growl stopped them dead in their tracks. It sounded like a guard dog. Suddenly from under one of the work benches, a metal dog shot out at them, barking furiously. It was a robot, but it sounded so life-like that Triple 'O' Seven was tempted to send it on its way with a kick.

"Stay Rover!" shouted U as he came to meet them. "Hello there, P, and you must be Triple 'O' Seven. Very happy to meet you."

"You, too, U," said Triple 'O'. "What I mean is, I'm happy to meet you. These code names are driving me crazy."

U laughed and Triple 'O' Seven took an instant liking to him. He was young and sandy haired with a pair of spectacles balanced on the end of his nose. His white lab coat was torn in several places, and six or seven pens stuck out of his pocket. He always seemed to be carrying a clipboard. Triple 'O' Seven supposed that this man was capable of anything; he seemed to love what he was doing.

"This is an early prototype for a robotic guard dog," U explained, pointing at the animal. "By the time I finish, and there is another model at the back which is much more life-like, you won't be able to tell the difference between robot and dog. It'll have hair, and move just like a real dog. Even this model has voice-activated photoelectric cells that enable the robot's computer to register its master's voice. For instance, tell it to go away.''

P gave a nod of his head to Triple 'O' Seven, indicating that he should tell the robot dog to go. Triple 'O' Seven felt kind of foolish.

"Go, Rover. Go sit." The dog did not move but a stream of yellow liquid fell to the floor. "The dog peed!" exclaimed Triple 'O' Seven.

"Well," said U, grinning, "it looks like there is still some work to do on the computer. I think it picked up your voice as saying 'Rover, go shit'. A little adjustment is all that's necessary." U gave it a sharp kick that sent it disappearing beneath the work benches and a howl came from the robot. "Come along and I'll give you the tour."

The first bench was full of electronic equipment that U said included an almost-complete laser gun. He tried to explain the workings of such a weapon but it was beyond the rudimentary levels of understanding of both Triple 'O' Seven and P. They both just nodded and made the appropriate sounds of understanding.

As they were going to the next bench, Triple 'O' Seven bent down to pick up what looked like a pile of dog shit. "This is amazing," he said to P. "Look at this, it's just like the real thing. It even smells like dog shit. How do you get this to come out of the robot?" he asked U.

"I don't," U replied.

"What!"

"I'm afraid that's the real stuff. Happy! Happy!" he called sternly. An aging dog approached the three of them, its head held low and tail wagging very slowly from side to side. "This is my dog, Happy," said U. He scolded the dog for pooping on the floor while Triple 'O' Seven looked for somewhere to clean up. He found an old rag and a sink where he washed and dried his hands, and felt very foolish when he rejoined the other two men.

"Now," said U. "This is what I have for you." He pulled a walnut case from a cupboard and flipped the silver locks. The case was the size of a briefcase. "When things start getting rough, this is all you should need." Both P and Triple 'O' Seven looked over his shoulder to see the contents of the case.

"For your tummy," said U, pulling a small vial of twelve pills from a pocket in the lining. "Not only will you have a good feeling in your tummy when you are killing people, you will have a good feeling all over when you take one of these babies. What they do is increase the level of adrenalin in the body whilst removing, or should I say, putting on hold, that part of your brain which controls emotions. In other words, you will become the most efficient, cold-blooded killer or fighting machine the world has ever known. That, at least, is the theory; they have never been tried before, except on animals."

"What kind of animals?" asked Triple 'O' Seven.

"Goldfish." He continued on before Triple 'O' could ask him anything further about the goldfish. "Now, from my experiments, I know that the pills will work but I must say there may be some side effects that I don't know about. So, to go along with the pills, you need the perfect weapon." He lifted up a red velvet cloth to reveal a gleaming pistol. "This weapon may not look different from any other large pistol, but watch this." He lifted it from the case and led the way to a target range. At the far end were some life-size dummy figures. "Those dummies are made especially for me out of concrete reinforced with one-inch rebar steel. The bullets for this gun are very small and allow for tremendous rapid fire capabilites; in fact almost one thousand rounds per minute when on automatic, or single rounds if you choose.''

U expertly pulled the magazine from the butt of the pistol and put some of the small B.B.-sized bullets into his hand.

"Tiny, aren't they? But they have a plutonium charge which gives them incredible powers of destruction. The bullets are very expensive, Triple 'O' Seven, so use them sparingly." He reloaded the gun. "Now, watch. Single shot first." He squeezed the trigger.

"Holy shit!" Both P and Triple 'O' Seven said the words at the same time. The gun had hardly made any noise at all yet the first concrete dummy had exploded to smithereens. All that was left was a piece of steel wire sticking upwards from a concrete stump.

"And now we put it on automatic. Ready, gentlemen?'' With a squeeze of the trigger which lasted for only a fraction of a second, U swept the sights of the gun across the three remaining targets, all of which exploded like the first one. U smiled, satisfied that he had awed them into silence. "There is a digital counter built into the stock which will show you how many rounds were fired." U pointed out the digital counter.

"That's amazing," said Triple 'O'. "What else does it do?''

"Well, besides killing enemy agents, it also does *this*." U suddenly whirled on P and Triple 'O' Seven. His eyes had clouded over and there was a sinister smile on his face. "Up against the wall. Both of you. Quick!''

"What's the meaning of this, U?" stammered P.

Both P and Triple 'O' Seven were completely taken aback by this sudden turn of events. With their hands held high, they backed up until they were against the wall.

"I demand an explanation!" shouted P.

Viciously, U rammed the end of the gun barrel into P's mouth. "This will shut you up. I've always wanted to do this." Now there was a mad look to U's face. P was very scared. His eyes were getting larger and larger.

"Bite the barrel," gritted U. "Bite it hard."

P bit down on the end of the barrel as hard as he could. To his surprise, the barrel snapped off. U doubled up with laughter and P began chewing the piece of barrel that was in his mouth.

"What the hell?" Triple 'O' Seven didn't know what was going on.

"Oh! That was a good one," laughed U. "The amazing thing about this gun is that it is made of chocolate. A special hard mixture that contains enough protein and water to let an agent survive, in desert or jungle, for weeks! That's why the barrel is so long."

P and Triple 'O' looked at U as he sprawled against one of the work benches and laughed uncontrollably, eyes watering.

"Not a bad flavour," said P, examining the gun more closely.

"Triple 'O' Seven said nothing: he was starting to have second thoughts about liking U.

P seemed to have recovered and was enjoying the chocolate as they followed the still-giggling U to the door.

"You will be issued the case, pills, and pistol before you leave," U said to Triple 'O' Seven. They ignored P, who was preoccupied with some pieces of metal on a nearby bench, looking for more chocolate.

"So, you're off to Los Angeles, Seven."

"Yes, in search of Pussy Love."

"Yes, of course....Still, it's the only clue we have."

As they shook hands, P shrieked in pain. He had just broken one of his teeth chomping on a set of pliers.

Triple 'O' Seven was fully briefed when he left for Los Angeles the next day. He did not see the headlines in the *Daily Express* telling the tragic story of how the death of a pedestrian from an umbrella stab wound in the back had somehow started a chain of events that had seen forty-six people admitted to hospital in one of the largest traffic accidents in the history of London.

Chapter Eight

WASHINGTON, D.C.

"Gentlemen, I hope you have a good reason for calling a meeting at one-thirty in the morning, otherwise I will be very annoyed."

The President of the United States put a hand up to his head and swept the tousled hair from his eyes. He surveyed the six men before him. They were all powerful men who between them decided the day-to-day operations of the United States. Higgins, Secretary of State, had obviously been delegated spokesman.

"Mr. President, I, that is, we, including the C.I.A., believe that this is a matter of national importance. It's difficult to explain, but...."

"God-damn it!" snapped the President. "For Christ's sake, Henry, spit it out."

The other five men suddenly burst into expressions of desperation as each one tried to blurt out the story.

"Stop!" shouted the President, quelling the outburst. "All of you, sit down. Only moments ago I was in the middle of watching a rerun of one of my old western movies when I get the call to come to the Oval Office for a meeting of national urgency. I arrive to find six of my top men close to a state of panic." He paused. "You haven't found out that the networks are going to stop showing my films, have you?"

"No, Mr. President, I'm afraid it's far worse than that."

There was a flash of fire in the eyes of the President as he listened to the reply of his Secretary of Defense. He wondered what could possibly be worse than depriving the American public of the joy and pleasure of watching their President in superb cinematic dramas that showed how good he was at everything from shooting up bad guys to caring for monkeys.

"Start from the beginning," said the President.

Henry Higgins cleared his throat and started to tell the story. "Mr. President, in the last few hours it was brought to our attention that the country is on the verge of economic disaster."

"You mean the film industry is going on strike again?" said the alarmed President.

"No, sir, I mean that every industry in this country is collapsing. A statistician with the Statistics Bureau was running a routine computer check on productivity and completing a study of work hours in the labour force. Over the last month, half the entire work force of the United States has been absent from their jobs. The results were checked and rechecked. Absenteeism is increasing at an incredible rate. Unless this is stopped, no one in this country is going to be working within a month, or maybe sooner. This means the total collapse of the entire country."

"Good God! What will those Commies stoop to next?" said the President, hitting the top of his desk.

Henry Higgins looked at the other men before continuing.

104

"We're not sure it is the Commies, Sir."

"What!" exclaimed the President. "Good God, man! Do you realize what you are saying? You are going against American tradition when you say the Commies are not responsible for our problems."

"I know that, Sir," agreed Higgins, "but we can find no evidence to substantiate that line of thinking."

"Make some up. Make up some evidence. Give me a good reason to nuke the lot of them, and our problems will be over." The President waved his hands and smiled with pleasure at the idea.

"I know we have done that before," said Higgins, "but it seems that the same thing is happening in Russia, not to mention England and Japan, and all of Europe. We've just notified England in the last hour. The Russians are blaming us. Japan is blaming us, and the Europeans are blaming everyone."

"Those damned Italians and Spanish guys are probably the ones stirring up all the shit in Europe," said the President. "As soon as anything goes wrong, they are the first to panic. The only good thing to come out of that part of the world in the last fifty years is the Clint Eastwood westerns."

"This could mean the start of World War Three," said the Secretary of Defense.

"A good war never hurt anybody. It's good for the economy, look how successful all those war films were."

Higgins looked at the other five men who had come to see the President. All of them wore blank expressions. Privately, he wondered if the President was in full control of his senses, and able to think rationally. Then Higgins saw that he was expected to continue.

"We have assured the Russians that we are not to blame, but I don't think they believe us. We have no idea why this Global Absenteeism is occurring. We've tested the atmosphere, the water, and foods, all for contaminants, but so far, nothing. We only know that day after day, more and more people are just not working. Manufacturing plants, brokerage houses, every kind of business imaginable, are closing their doors. We have spoken to hundreds of workers. They say they don't care, they're tired and don't want to go to work.''

"Well, send out the army. Send the men to do boys' jobs," suggested the President.

"Sir," Higgins cleared his throat again. "We don't have much of an army left, either."

"What?" shouted the President. "What do you mean?"

"The same thing is happening with our soldiers; over forty percent of our entire armed forces are staying home with their wives and families, or girlfriends. We can't control it."

"The military police. Get the military police to slap them all in jail," said the President.

"We don't have any military police to speak of. The same thing has happened to them," said Higgins.

The President, who had gotten up from the table, sat back down again. The seriousness of the situation had finally hit home. The men in the Oval Office sat quietly watching the President drumming his fingers on the top of the table. He was losing his country. He would be remembered as the President who fucked up the whole fucking country. He knew that these men were expecting some leadership from him. He *was* their leader; he had to think of something quickly, to inspire them. They were all watching him, waiting for the words of a leader. He must not fail them! If the men at the top who ruled this great nation started to panic, the end would be near.

The President looked at the men and slowly rose from his chair. He pulled his blue dressing gown about him and re-tied the belt, put his hands behind his back, and paced the length of the room. Silence dragged on for an eternity. The President was racking his brain for some words of wisdom.

Suddenly it came to him.

"Anybody like some buttered popcorn?"

•

"Bloody hell!" said the Prime Minister. She held the phone between her head and left shoulder and struggled to light a cigarette. She had just been informed that two-thirds of the English workforce were in fact not working and that the country was on the verge of collapse. What really annoyed her was not the fact that two-thirds of the workforce was absent, but that the information had been relayed to her from the United States. Obviously they were keeping information on the English economic situation and were on top of it more than her own staff. There was nothing unusual about no one working in England, the bloody unions were always striking everything. "Bloody hell!" she said again, when told that the unions had nothing to do with the absenteeism. Within a week, if the trend did not reverse itself, the country would be in a state of chaos and the economy at a standstill. Not to mention National Defence. The country would be completely vulnerable.

After listening for a few more minutes, she replaced the telephone into its cradle. She sat up in bed, deep in thought. Looking at her watch, she saw that it was almost nine a.m. Her husband entered the bedroom carrying a breakfast tray with bacon and eggs and a small rose in a petite vase.

"Breakfast is ready," he said.

"What did you say?"

"I'm sorry, Mrs. Prime Minister. Breakfast is ready, Prime Minister." He bowed his head, expecting another tongue-lashing from his wife. He loved to be dominated. He was dressed in maid's attire with a short black dress and white apron. The Prime Minister leapt from the bed and smashed the tray out of his hands. It flew through the air and landed face down on the carpet. She slapped her husband's face. A red welt showed up through the makeup. His eyes began to sparkle.

"Get me P," she commanded.

"Pee, Mrs. Prime Minister?"

"Yes, P."

"Oh! Yes, Prime Minister." He was now very excited. This was going to be a fun morning. He loved to serve his wife this way. It took all the stress out of being the Prime Minister's husband. Within minutes, he came running back into the room carrying a small sample bottle full of urine.

"What's that?" asked the Prime Minister.

"Pee," replied her husband, holding out the bottle.

The Prime Minister punched him in the stomach, doubling him over. She then brought up her knee into his face, which sent him careening backwards to land sprawling in a corner of the room. "You incompetent!" she shrieked. "I ask for P and you bring me pee. Bloody hell! What is this country coming to?" She walked out of the room. She must speak with P, but first a shower. She always thought well in the shower.

The Prime Minister did do a lot of thinking in the shower. This was all the time she needed: she resolved to handle this problem as she had handled the Falklands. Maybe she would come out of it with the people solidly behind her. First, though, she had to get all the facts. She had to talk to P. Feeling in a much better frame of mind, she finished her shower and shave, pampered herself with oils, liberally sprayed herself with underarm deodorant, and went back to check on her husband. He was on his hands and knees cleaning up the breakfast. She felt a sudden pang of affection for him and restrained herself from giving him her usual goodbye kick. Instead, she cupped his face between her hands and raised him up from the floor. "I want you, now," she whispered.

"Yes, Prime Minister," he whispered back, flinching a

little in case she was setting him up for her goodbye kick. He allowed himelf to be pulled to the bed.

•

"I have been trying, your Majesty. I have been trying to get her for three hours, ever since we had the opportunity to disseminate the information." P listened as the Queen told him again that it was a matter of national urgency.

He had actually been trying to reach the Prime Minister for the last five hours, but he didn't dare mention this to the Queen. The Prime Minister's phone was busy. He imagined that she was on a conference call to the U.S. or Japan.

Truscott of the Yard sat opposite him. Since receiving the information, neither of them had come up with any idea as to what was causing the incredible lack of motivation in the English workforce. The ramifications were enormous. The phone to P's office had not stopped ringing as more and more information was fed to him. Apparently, this was not happening just in England, but in all of the major industrialized countries of the world as well.

Truscott sat watching P as he answered the phone. Smoke from his pipe made a lazy path to the open window and was suddenly sucked out as the draught caught it and whisked it away into the open air. Truscott had been in the office since the news had come in at seven-thirty. A quick assessment of the information and an earlier talk with Her Majesty had set the investigative wheels in motion. For those few people who were aware of the problem, it was a real crisis.

"God-damn! Sometimes the Royals drive me crazy," P said, slamming the phone down. "I don't know why they don't just stick to raising horses or something, instead of meddling in our affairs. The time I have wasted listening to her tell me what I already know! I could have been doing something useful."

"Anything new?" asked Truscott, taking another deep puff of his pipe.

"Not a blessed thing. No one knows anything except that we have a real problem, as do all of the major economic powers. I wonder if these killings and so on have anything to do with what's going on? I suppose I should try and get in touch with Triple 'O' Seven."

"Triple 'O' Seven. Who's he?" asked Truscott.

"Oh, you don't know him. He's a new agent who came in yesterday. I've just sent him out on the company plane, heading for Los Angeles. He should be arriving any time now." P glanced at his watch and, lost in thought, nervously chewed on the end of the pencil. He grimaced in pain as he hit the nerve endings of where there had once been a tooth.

"Well, I think that if no new developments are in the offing, I will get back to the Yard. Call me if anything new pops up." Truscott reached for his coat and walked out of the office, leaving P feeling the gap in his teeth with the end of his finger.

•

Refreshed after spending almost ten hours in the jumbo jet with Candy, Honey and Sugar, Triple 'O' Seven strolled jauntily down a corridor of Los Angeles airport, towards the exit. The hot air hit him like a sledge hammer when he stepped out into the glorious California day. The airport was teeming with people who swarmed in and out of the doors, arriving from and leaving for their various flights to all parts of the world. Triple 'O' Seven looked about for his contact.

He heard the beep of a car horn and looked to see where it was coming from. About fifty feet away he saw a blue-speckled dune buggy double parked. A young man was waving at him.

Triple 'O' walked over to the dune buggy and watched the

young man give a naughty sign to a cab driver who was complaining about him blocking the lane.

"Hey, man, I'm Timmy Baby, how you doin'?" He extended a hand which Triple 'O' Seven shook as he settled into the passenger seat of the car. Timmy was about thirty years old. He had short hair and was dressed in cut-offs and a vest. His tan was the result of a few days spent on the beaches of the California coast.

"Want some?" said Timmy, lighting up a joint. The heady aroma of the smoke filled Seven's nostrils.

"Never touch the stuff," he replied. "Are you sure you can drive when you've smoked that stuff?"

"You ain't seen drivin' till you drive with me stoned, man. Y'know, it's almost like a cosmic experience. Y'know what I mean? Like totally."

The dune buggy took a sudden leap forward which threw Triple 'O' Seven back into his seat. The car wove in and out of traffic at breakneck speed, the tires squealing, as the car accelerated towards the highway.

Neither of them appeared to notice the red Corvette with blacked out windows following them a safe distance behind. A personalized licence plate with the word 'PUSSY' was partially covered with dust.

A large antenna started to rise from the back of the Corvette. Pussy Love, the beautiful blonde who had returned the briefcase to the C.I.A. agent, realized that the dune buggy was heading away from Los Angeles towards the desert roads that led to Las Vegas. The car was obviously heading for the young agent's house in the desert, and she would need help.

"Zero Four Niner, break Two Zero." The radio crackled as Pussy's words were transmitted and scrambled.

"Go ahead, Zero Four Niner." The radio voice emphasized her code number.

"Request assistance of Desert Kill squad. Target heading

111

east on Highway number fifteen. They should be turning off at Calico in about twenty minutes' time. Remember, our orders are to kill Triple 'O' Seven.'' Pussy turned to her daughter, who sat beside her playing with a small doll. ''I think we should go and watch this, darling, and then when it's all over, we'll go and get some ice cream.''

Chapter Nine

HAWAII

There are many species of birds which inhabit the Hawaiian chain of islands. Birds that glide in seemingly effortless flight on warm air currents.

The Lesser Noddy Tern, indigenous to the Hawaiian Islands, is one of the more common. It is an orange-coloured bird with long slender wings. It competes with others such as the Sooty Tern, a slightly larger cousin, and the Wedge-tailed Shearwater, for nesting space. The birds in their thousands scream, dart, and fight for territorial rights to a small piece of rock on which to lay their eggs and look after their young.

Just off the east coast of Oahu is a large bird sanctuary strictly policed by the Department of Wildlife and Preservation of the State of Hawaii. The sanctuary is on an uninhabited island known as Manana Island.

Manana Island was perhaps even more protected by the Department because of the rare bird known as Bulwer's Petrel.

The Petrel is a very shy and gentle little bird rarely seen except at sea. The adults come to the nesting ground only at dusk and fly straight into a burrow, where they stay until dawn the next day. Slowly, through careful work, the Department charged with their protection was increasing the numbers of these rare birds.

Any application to visit the Island is subject to the most critical evaluation which determines the beneficial, educational or scientific merits of the proposed entry.

Apart from State Department officials, there had been only two applications approved during the last five years. Both of those individuals—one a resident of Hawaii who owned a small bar on Molokai; the other, Joseph Martini, a C.I.A. agent, each excellent and well known bird watchers and photographers—were now dead. This hadn't seemed to faze the birds, who still wheeled overhead and called angrily to each other, trying to make themselves heard over the noise of the pounding surf.

Occasionally over the last few months, the nesting birds had suddenly raised their heads as one and stared at each other, fear in their eyes, worry clouding their tiny foreheads. Something was happening that they did not understand. There were tremors underneath them. They poised, ready to lift themselves into the air to escape any possible danger, but the moments always passed, and as the tremors became more frequent, the birds became used to them.

Far below the birds, in the very core of Manana Island, a huge production facility had been hewn from the rock. Bloh Jobb had chosen this site because human access to the surface of the island was strictly controlled. He could expect very few visitors, and his private entrance was hidden by the ocean waves: atomic-powered mini-subs could come and go as they pleased. But for Jobb, the most pleasing aspect of this location was the bird sanctuary above him—no one in his right mind would ever imagine that an operation which would result in control of the entire world would be run from beneath tons and tons of bird shit. Bloh Jobb had devised the perfect scheme. It was so cunningly simple that he had laughed when the idea first came to him.

Dr. Yes and Dr. Maybe had scoffed at his plan and wanted nothing to do with it, but as he put to good use the financial resources General Bretzky had so foolishly provided, the twins had changed their minds. They were now *also* delighted with the results.

However, Bloh Jobb had not told them everything. He had kept back the fact that he was double-crossing his financial backers in Russia. He had so far managed to keep a lot of the information from Irma Klogg so that she could provide only very vague reports for General Bretzky. She was a pain in the neck, the way she followed him about and leaned over his shoulder all the time. He'd also noticed that she was touching him a lot more; nothing obvious, but she kept brushing against him. His cat, which he always carried, had scratched her twice on the face leaving claw marks down one side. Klogg hated the cat with a passion and he knew she would, in time, try to get even.

But Bloh Jobb was impressed by her efficiency: she had dispatched the last two visitors to the island. A precautionary move, just in case they had noticed any of the tremors as he had built the huge cavern to house the factory and living quarters.

Once the factory was fully operational, the first phase of Bloh Jobb's Master Plan had gone into effect. Slowly and surely, the operation had progressed without a hitch. With the elimination of Dr. Lawrence, the final component of Phase One had been neatly put in place, and already the results were more than he dared hope for! It would have gone on unnoticed for months except for the U.S. government's Statistics Bureau. Some two-bit government statistician had discovered the alarming rise in absenteeism among the workforce and had, according to his source, informed the President. Still, thought Bloh Jobb, Phase One was complete and there was absolutely nothing they could do about it.

This day, Bloh Jobb was furious with Dr. Yes and Dr. Maybe. In a breakfast conversation, they had repeatedly made vulgar jokes about his relationship with Irma Klogg. Bloh Jobb was so furious that he did not trust himself to meet the twins again unless his killing lust has been appeased somewhat. He had ordered Irma Klogg to find him some new karate experts for one of his deadly aerobic 'workouts'. Six men had been shipped into the underground base at once, and all six had been dispatched within thirty minutes as Bloh Jobb vented his anger on them. He needed the twins for a while longer, but as soon as they had served their purpose, he would personally find it a pleasure to snap their necks and listen to the bones in their spines being crushed in his grip.

In Bloh Jobb's luxurious subterranean office, Irma Klogg watched the three men and tried to suppress a thin smile; she had observed Jobb's morning workout. She knew that Bloh Jobb thought she was old and stupid, but she hadn't played all her cards yet and felt a shiver of sexual excitement at the thought of possessing his magnificent body. Irma knew her reports to General Bretzky were vague, but she also knew that the huge black man had planned a double-cross of her old boss. In her years with General Bretzky, she had seen many men get greedy and try to do what Bloh Jobb was doing. The success rate to date was nil. All of the men who had tried to cheat Bretzky had died terrible deaths. If she blew the whistle on Bloh Jobb before his plan was ready, then he, too, would be disposed of by the General. But she knew that Bloh Jobb was probably the one man with the right combination of brains, imagination and courage to pull it off, and what a couple they would make together!

As she watched the twins, she felt a sincere disgust. Even

so, it was hard to suppress another smile. She knew that it was she, Irma Klogg, who held the real key to whether the incredible plan of Bloh Jobb would succeed or fail.

Bloh Jobb's voice was icy as he spoke. "If you think that General Bretzky is a hard man to please, wait until you see me. Any more crude jokes concerning myself or...Miss Klogg, and I will personally tear you apart limb by limb. I will force you, Dr. Yes, to eat your own flesh until you totally disappear."

Irma Klogg stared approvingly at the muscular giant. He was stroking the cat so hard she thought its spine would break.

"That's disgusting," said Dr. Yes.

"Most self-serve food is," replied Bloh Jobb.

"Don't go threatening my brother," said Dr. Maybe, in a high feminine voice and with a swish of his wrist. "What happened was a freak thing. You threaten us and we both go back to New York, right now. Who needs this? Do you think living under this island of bird shit is fun?"

Irma Klogg intervened. "Gentlemen, gentlemen, please. There's no need for language like that when there's a lady present."

"Where?" said Dr. Maybe. Irma Klogg gave him a cold stare and continued.

"Everybody has been working very hard, and I think that you have all done a tremendous job in putting the plan into effect so quickly." She could see that the praise fed their egos. "I suggest that we all have a recess; some food and drink before Bloh Jobb heads back to Florida." The suggestion was well-timed and defused their volatile and hostile feelings.

Bloh Jobb looked at his watch. He was not really interested in eating, but he recognized that Klogg had saved a possibly dangerous situation with no loss of face for anyone. He was counting on time being on his side for his plan to work. All he needed now was a bit more time.

The four of them walked from the spacious office and into the heart of the operation. There were almost one hundred scientists working round the clock for Bloh Jobb, and they paused to watch the men and women work. It was a grand sight. Bloh Jobb felt Klogg touch his arm, and the cat hissed at her. He looked at Klogg and noticed that she was trying to draw him out of the twins' hearing range.

"What is it, Miss Klogg?"

"I just thought you should know of a potential problem. I hope it's been taken care of by now. We received word that a new agent has been assigned to investigate the deaths of the C.I.A. agent and the owner of the bar on Molokai."

"Ah! Our source has come through again. Who is the agent?"

"His name is Triple 'O' Seven."

"Where is he now?"

"Near Los Angeles."

"And what are you doing about this Triple 'O' Seven?" asked Bloh Jobb.

"Pussy Love and her daughter are still under our control and working for us. How easy it is for men to succumb to a beautiful girl." There was more than a hint of resentment in her voice. Bloh Jobb, recognizing the beauty of Pussy Love, and how effective it could be, had had both her and her daughter brainwashed to follow all their orders. She had proven to be most valuable. Bloh Jobb made a mental note to reinforce her programming in the near future.

"Good. When her mission is accomplished, I want to know. Make sure that you keep in touch with our units in Los Angeles. I want you to come with me to the base in Florida as soon as we make sure that everything here is perfect."

Irma fell into step behind Bloh Jobb and let a smile spread across her face. Perhaps he didn't realize it, but he had just said 'we'. Again, she felt the sexual tingling. It would not be long now before she had her man. For a brief moment, she wondered if this Triple 'O' Seven had been killed yet. She looked at her watch. She would soon know.

•

As the dune buggy left Los Angeles, the air became clean and sweet. It felt good as it swept back Triple 'O' Seven's hair. He relaxed and watched the scenery go by.

Timmy Baby had plugged in a tape of an unrecognizable band and turned up the volume. Two large speakers, more like those found in someone's living room, were wired to the roll bar at the back of the car, and blared at full volume.

Timmy Baby was high on wacky-backy but this did not seem to hinder his ability to drive. In fact, his reflexes seemed razor sharp. Triple 'O' Seven had remarked on his quick reflexes and Timmy had explained that, living in the desert, the senses were honed. His eyesight and senses of smell and hearing had improved immensely because they were not continuously bombarded by the stench and noise of the city.

The dune buggy turned off the highway and onto a narrow dirt road which petered out until it was no more than a trail. After a few miles, even the trail vanished. Spirals of dust were lifted by the desert breeze and the odd clump of sagebrush blew across their path.

Timmy Baby brought the dune buggy to a stop on the crest of a rise and turned off his stereo. He surveyed the Old West ghost town that lay before him.

"This is where you live?" asked Triple 'O' Seven.

"This is it," replied Timmy. "What do you think of it?"

"Well, it's smaller than New York. What do you do for action?"

"You'd be surprised. You want action, you got it. But first, I think you better take a couple of drags on this."

Timmy was busy rolling another joint.

"No thanks, I don't smoke the stuff."

"Make an exception this time. Here." He handed the lighted joint to Triple 'O' Seven and started to do up his racing harness seatbelts. "You'd better do yours up as well."

Triple 'O' Seven was sucking the smoke into his lungs. An immediate wave of light-headedness rushed over him. "Why the seatbelts? I thought we were here....Oh boy! This stuff is good."

"We are here, but I think we have company."

"Oh!" Triple 'O' Seven looked down at the old wooden buildings. He could see nothing that alarmed him. The place looked deserted. A piece of corrugated tin roofing rocked backwards and forwards in the wind making an eerie noise as it slapped against a metal sign, but that was the only noise or sign of movement he could see. "How do you know?"

"There are some engines running down there. They're muffled, but I can hear them."

Triple 'O' Seven strained to detect the noise of the engines but could hear nothing.

"I think that you should get your gun ready, too," said Timmy, taking a revolver from beneath the seat. It was a huge weapon, a Magnum .44 that had been adapted to handle a larger bullet. He grabbed an ammunition belt from behind the seat and slung it over his shoulders, and removed a panel from the inside of the dune buggy door to reveal a rack of hand grenades. A button was pushed and from the front of the car, two panels slid back to reveal the muzzles of two machine guns. A flick of a switch armed them.

"Wow! That's pretty impressive," said Triple 'O' Seven. "What do you have?"

"Oh, yes." Triple 'O' Seven had been so engrossed watching Timmy that he had completely forgotten about his weapon. He snapped open the wooden case. "Well, here goes." He popped open the little plastic pill box and took one of the small white pills.

"What the hell are those?" asked Timmy.

"I'm not really sure. I was told they would make me a mean fighting machine, maybe."

"Maybe?"

"Well, they've only been tested on goldfish."

"Goldfish?"

"Goldfish."

"They must work then." Timmy started to laugh. Triple 'O' flipped back the red velvet cloth covering his gun, and Timmy whistled. "What the hell is that?"

"A new type of pistol. Quite impressive, actually. Well, are we ready to go?"

They were both buckled in tight to the dune buggy. Timmy revved up the engine and pressed another two switches.

"Super charger and positraction," explained Timmy. "We will also have to do something about the red Corvette that's been following us since we left the airport."

Triple 'O' Seven looked behind him but again could see and hear nothing.

"One ridge back," explained Timmy, taking a last puff of the joint. He passed it to Triple 'O' who also took one last puff and threw away the remains. "Feel anything with the pills?"

"Not yet. But this wacky-backy is sure doing strange things."

Timmy slammed down the accelerator and the dune buggy shot toward the main street of the ghost town. Sand spewed up from the huge tires as they gripped and propelled the car forward at breakneck speed.

A roar of engines filled the town as they approached.

"There's ten of them," shouted Timmy.

Triple 'O' Seven didn't question his statement.

A humming sound came from the engine as the turbo charger kicked in. The car leapt forward again, forcing both

121

of them back into their seats. Triple 'O' Seven let out a whoop.

"Are the pills starting to work?" shouted Timmy.

"Yes."

"That's great."

"I don't think so," said Triple 'O'.

"Why?"

"I feel like having sex with a goldfish!"

"Oh, jeez!"

"I'm only joking," laughed Triple 'O' Seven. "Yahoo!"

Before long, the first enemy vehicle appeared: a white dune buggy with a powerful engine came roaring out of an alley. Timmy pressed the button on the steering wheel and the machine guns barked into action. A second dune buggy followed the first and they both tore up the sandy main street heading straight at them, spraying bullets from automatic weapons. Triple 'O' Seven took a bead on the second vehicle as the machine guns of Timmy's dune buggy found their mark. Both cars in front of them erupted into flame with a loud explosion.

"Wow!" shouted Timmy. "That's quite a gun. Hang on!" Timmy spun the steering wheel as two more enemy dune buggies roared into the street behind them and from one side. Timmy raced for the old saloon and Triple 'O' let out another whoop as the dune buggy suddenly became airborne and went crashing through the walls of the old building. The car continued across the floor of the saloon and through the back wall. Timmy spun the wheel again and charged down an alley coming back into main street.

"Allow me," yelled Triple 'O' Seven. He aimed at the first car, fired, and then quickly drew a bead on the second. They both burst into flames. The other cars had disappeared into the side alleys of the town.

"Four down, six to go. Hang on. There's another one to our left."

The enemy dune buggy had roared up behind them. The passenger in the car unleashed a stream of bullets from a sub-machine gun. The bullets pinged off the body of Timmy's vehicle. Triple 'O' Seven had thought it was fiberglass, but it was obviously bullet-proof metal. Restrained by their seat belts, they couldn't stand to return the fire.

"Give me a grenade," shouted Triple 'O'.

Timmy grabbed a grenade from the rack, pulled the pin with his teeth, and handed it over. Triple 'O' Seven counted to four and threw it at the dune buggy just as it came along-side them. The grenade landed in the lap of the driver. A look of horror came over his face as the grenade fell to the floor. In a panic, he cranked the wheel of the dune buggy. It careened over on one side and slid into an old building that looked like it had once been a hardware store. The dune buggy disap-peared into the dark interior and then suddenly reappeared as the grenade blew it and the building apart. A huge ball of flame swept upwards and out across the street.

Timmy spun the car around and stopped. He was at the end of the street. They both looked down to the far end of the street.

Facing them were the five remaining dune buggies. They were painted white and each had two people in it wearing white uniforms and white helmets.

Timmy pulled a cassette tape from the case and plugged it into the stereo. It was an old western tune that reminded Tri-ple 'O' Seven of the film, *High Noon*.

Timmy pressed lightly on the accelerator and they ad-vanced slowly. At the other end of the street, the five white dune buggies did the same. Eyes strained on both sides to see who would make the first move.

The music continued to blare out and fill the street. Triple 'O' Seven wanted a drink of water. He wondered if it had anything to do with the pill he had taken. For some reason, he kept thinking about goldfish. He shook his head and concentrated on the matter at hand.

He sighted his gun on one of the dune buggies and started to squeeze the trigger.

"Now!" shouted Timmy. At the same time, he floored it and pressed the firing button on the steering wheel. The dune buggy shot forward. Triple 'O' Seven fired and they both had the pleasure of seing two more white dune buggies explode before the others replied with a hail of fire.

For good measure, as Timmy turned off the main road into a small alley, he lobbed another grenade. The vehicles speeding towards them managed to avoid the blast, and now the three remaining dune buggies roared down the alley after Timmy and Triple 'O' Seven, guns blazing. On the back street, the sand over the years had almost reached the rooftops of the decrepit buildings. Timmy gunned the engine and the buggy shot up the side of a dune and flew into the air, travelling some fifty feet before thumping down into the next sand dune. The three buggies chasing them did the same thing, and looked like a mechanical ballet flying through the air.

Timmy spun the car around again in a different direction and roared towards the crest of another dune. At the same time, he passed a grenade to Triple 'O' Seven. As they flew into the air, Triple 'O' realized that he could drop the grenade directly into the car beneath them. Timmy successfully managed the manoeuvre with uncanny skill. The grenade exploded while they were still in the air and the dune buggy below them was nothing but a ball of flame.

"Well, I think it's time to get Big Baby out," shouted Timmy.

"What's that?"

"Wait and see."

Pulling the dune buggy around, he sped back into town. At the far end of the main street, he pushed a button on the dash. It was a garage door sensor. An old building with a camouflaged door was suddenly ahead. As the door lifted, Timmy pressed another button and a deafening roar filled the garage. Triple 'O' Seven couldn't believe what he saw. It was a gigantic truck like those used in an open pit mine.

"Quick, jump in," said Timmy, running from the dune buggy.

At first Triple 'O' Seven couldn't figure out how to climb up the side of the truck. It was almost fifteen feet high. Timmy was already in the cab and pushed a button that made a retractable ladder appear. Triple 'O' clambered up. The huge engine throbbed with power, and the truck vibrated with wild energy.

It leapt forward from the garage and smashed into an old wooden building. Splinters flew everywhere as the tires crunched through the walls.

"They're coming down the back street," Timmy shouted. "I think I can cut them off."

As the truck crashed through the last wall of the building, one of the two remaining dune buggies was showered with debris. Without slowing down, the truck crushed the dune buggy and its occupants beneath its huge tires. The second and last dune buggy, caught by surprise, screeched to a halt in front of the massive truck. There was no way for the driver to avoid the awesome destructive power of the vehicle in front of him. Triple 'O' Seven could see the two occupants scramble to undo their seatbelts and run from the buggy, but it was too late.

A whoosh of flame from the front of the truck engulfed the dune buggy and the occupants. The dune buggy exploded and disappeared. Only a swirl of dust remained.

"I think that's the lot of them," said Timmy.

Triple 'O' Seven opened the door and jumped from the truck. "You get supper ready and I'll go after the Corvette."

"What would you like to eat?"

"Goldfish. Barbecued goldfish," he shouted over his

shoulder as he ran back to the garage and the dune buggy.

Triple 'O' Seven leapt into the dune buggy, wheeled it round and headed off towards the ridge. He saw a flash of red as the Corvette made a quick turn and sped for the highway.

Pussy Love had seen the total destruction of the Desert Kill Squad and put her foot to the accelerator. A plume of sand trailed from the car as it fish-tailed away. The dune buggy was in pursuit. She had failed in her mission to kill Triple 'O' Seven.

Chapter Ten

WASHINGTON

"Mr. President, I really don't think...."

"For Christ's sake, be quiet, Higgins. This is one of the best parts in the movie. Just shut your mouth and eat your popcorn."

Higgins threw up his arms in despair. None of them had left the Oval Office since the meeting had been called. The President in his wisdom had suggested that they all make themselves comfortable and enjoy their popcorn, and had had a television set brought in with some video tapes of his movies. Soon after, he had picked up the phone and ordered the maids to roll in a number of beds. The Oval Office now looked like an army barracks. Empty popcorn buckets were strewn about between the cots and they had been served until they were all full. The President seemed to have an infinite amount of room in his stomach for what was obviously his favorite snack.

A wait-and-eat attitude had been taken by the President. The telephone linking him with the other major powers around the world was snuggled in around his feet.

The President slapped his knee with glee as he laughed at one of his favorite scenes with the chimp. "Did you see that?" he said, pointing at the television screen, totally absorbed. "Ha! That little monkey. What a scene stealer. By George! Every kid should have a pet monkey. Hey! That's not a bad idea." He turned to his advisors. "What do you think? We could pass a law through Congress that says every kid has to have a pet monkey sometime before puberty. Then we could initiate a special tax on bananas. When the kids grow too old to keep their monkeys, we could use them for experiments or something."

"Great idea, Mr. President. Maybe we could get the monkeys to form a new political party." Higgins looked at the other men in the room for some supporting laughter, but there was none. They knew that Higgins was treading on thin ice, making jokes about one of the President's favourite animals.

The President gave Higgins a withering stare. The tension in the room built as they all waited for the President to speak.

"Sarcasm is the lowest form of wit, Higgins. Now shut up and eat your popcorn."

"Yes, sir, Mr. President," said Higgins, aware that he'd gone too far.

The telephone rang, startling everyone. For a moment, the President looked at it. It rang again. He wiped his buttery fingers on his blue dressing gown and picked up the receiver. "This is the President of the United States speaking," he said, trying to pick a piece of popcorn from his teeth.

"What did you say?" came the reply.

The President, still with a finger in his mouth, didn't

realize that this made it very difficult for the calling party to understand him. "I said, 'This is the President of the United States speaking.' Who is this?"

"I can't understand a word the man says," P whispered to Truscott, placing his hand over the telephone. Truscott shrugged. "This is P in England, Mr. President."

"Who?"

"P, Sir."

The President covered the mouthpiece and turned to his men in the Oval Office. "Anyone here ever had any contact with P in England?"

"Is that some sort of sexual thing they do in England?" asked General Wollop, assistant to Higgins.

Everybody shrugged. "Have you ever seen any of my movies?" the President asked into the telephone.

"Yes, sir, I have. Very good," said P. He had seen one of the President's films but hadn't thought very much of it, however, a little flattery was always a good thing.

"Good man. Now then, let me get this straight. Your name is P?"

"P, Sir," confirmed P.

"God-damn it, man, what kind of name is that? You with some religious group or something?"

"No, sir. P is my code name with British Special Intelligence. I represent not only the Queen of England, but the Prime Minister." P sounded a little exasperated. He sometimes wished the code names could be thrown out of the window. He spent more time explaining his code name over the telephone than he did getting his message across.

"P, huh! That's a code name, right? That's not your real name?"

"No, sir. That is not my real name." P was starting to get a little testy now. "I don't think that any sane parent would give someone a real name like that. Mr. President, the Queen has commanded me to phone and tell you that

England is now in an official state of emergency. To compound matters, the Prime Minister and her husband have disappeared and the country is without a formal leader.''

"Tell him that we can only last about forty-eight hours before complete chaos destroys England," added Truscott.

"We feel that we have about forty-eight hours before total chaos destroys England, and probably less, if the Prime Minister remains missing," echoed P.

"Good God!" exclaimed the President loudly. Suddenly his staff members were all ears. They sat frozen, waiting for news of the latest disaster. The President was in an agitated state. He carried the telephone around the Oval Office repeating the words 'Good God' several times. "This is worse than cutting out the cartoon before the main feature," he muttered.

"Yes it is, sir," agreed P. "Mr. President, we have one hope. We feel that whatever is happening in our country and yours is somehow tied in with the killing of Professor Lawrence and a number of other killings that have taken place in the last little while. We don't know what the connection is, but we have one of our agents working on it right now.''

"An agent?"

"Yes, Mr. President. An agent named Triple 'O' Seven.''

"That's his code name?"

"No, sir, that's his real name.''

" 'Triple 'O' Seven' is his real name. What's his code name?"

"He doesn't have one, sir.''

"What's his present status?"

"We lost contact with him in Los Angeles, sir. He was supposed to have met an agent of yours called Timmy Baby.''

"Another code name, right?" asked the President. He smiled to himself, pleased that he was catching on to all this cloak and dagger stuff. It reminded him of the Bogart movies.

"Wrong, Sir."

"Wrong?" The smile disappeared from his face.

"Yes, sir. I'm afraid that's his real name, also."

"Well, where are they now?"

"They were supposed to drive to Calico and report from there," answered P.

"Calico. That's a code name, right?"

"Wrong, Sir. Calico is an old ghost town east of Los Angeles."

The President was starting to get a little annoyed now at not being able to guess what was coded and what was not. He brushed his hair back and snapped at P. "And?"

"They didn't go fishing," said P, exasperated with the slow mind of the President.

"What are they doing goin' fishin'?" shouted the President.

"That's code, Sir, for *report in*. They are late with a report. The only thing I can think of is that they've got themselves into a spot of trouble."

"Leave it to me," the President snapped. "What are those agents' names again?"

"Triple 'O' Seven and Timmy Baby."

"I'll take care of it. If those boys are onto something, they will have the might of the most powerful country in the world behind them. I will see to this personally." He turned to Higgins. "Higgins, get me Air Force One, and although I promised Nancy I would never wear them again, get my holster and six shooters out of the closet. P, I want you to keep in touch with me. I'm leaving for Calico right now to save those agents, Timmy 'O' Seven and Baby Triple."

"Triple 'O' Seven and Timmy Baby," corrected P.

"Whatever. Just leave it to the U.S. Cavalry." The President hung up the phone and turned to face his men.

131

"Men, there comes a time in every President's life when he has to make a decision of major importance. With Washington, it had something to do with chopping down a pear tree. With Jefferson, it was whether or not he could sit through an awful play. With Nixon, it was, well, I'm not sure what it was with Nixon. With Ford, it was whether or not to get a golf tournament named after him. Now, it's my turn. Out there in Calico are two brave men, two secret agents who may just have the solution to our problem. I have just heard that England is down the tubes. The Queen is running around like a chicken with its head cut off. Not only is it our duty to save our country, but it is also our duty to save our allies. Men! Today we ride!"

The men in the Oval Office had all stood to listen to the inspiring words of the President. All except Smith, Assistant Secretary of Agriculture, who remained on his cot.

"What's the matter with him?" asked the President. "He looks dead."

Higgins, who had just come back into the room carrying a studded gunbelt with two pearl-handled revolvers, stopped by Smith's bed. He quickly lifted the eyelids and let them fall.

"He looks dead because he *is* dead," said Higgins. "It looks like he choked to death on a piece of popcorn."

"Serves him right. After all, he grows the stuff, doesn't he?" The President strapped his gunbelt round his waist as he spoke. "Let's go, men." With a wave of his arm, he led them cheering out of the Oval Office and down the corridor. The President pulled Higgins aside and whispered in his ear. "First opportunity you get, Higgins, I want you to get hold of my agent and see if you can make a deal on the film rights for this story. I think it will make a fine movie."

P stared at the telephone, and then at Truscott, before replacing the receiver. "That has to be the strangest

132

telephone call I have ever made in my life. The President of the United States is a nut cake. A sagging, right-off-the-wall piece of wallpaper. A flake.''

"What did he say?" asked Truscott, stuffing his pipe and lighting it.

"I'm not really sure, something about the U.S. Cavalry going to rescue Triple 'O' Seven."

"Well, let's not worry about Triple 'O' Seven," said Truscott. "I think we should spend our energy trying to find out what happened to the Prime Minister."

"Of course, of course," agreed P, "but I can't help wondering what Triple 'O' Seven has gotten himself into. He was supposed to have reported in by now."

"C'mon, P," said Truscott, "let's go out for a breath of fresh air. It will do us both good."

"You're right. Let's go." P punched the intercom. "Mizzz Mummypenny, I want to be informed the moment there is any news from Triple 'O' Seven, the Prime Minister, or the President of the United States. In that order."

•

The sun was now scorching the desert sands around Calico. Triple 'O' Seven had found it relatively easy to drive the dune buggy to a position far ahead of the Corvette, and had placed himself so that he had a good view of the car as it sped towards him. He could knock it out at any time with his pistol, but right now that was the last thing he wanted to do. Whoever was driving the car was more than likely responsible for the attack on himself and Timmy. The car had followed them from the airport and had overseen the attack in Calico. Triple 'O' Seven wanted to talk to whoever was driving the car.

As the car raced towards him, a trail of dust spurting up from the rear wheels, Triple 'O' Seven took careful aim and fired. A burst of flame and sand showered the corvette on the driver's side, forcing it to swerve. Triple 'O' Seven took aim again and fired to the other side of the car. The driver swerved again, and headed directly towards him. Two more quick shots sent the flame and sand high into the sky. The driver now knew that a fiery death was near if the vehicle did not come to a halt immediately.

Triple 'O' Seven crouched, ready to jump aside if the driver dared to try and drive over him. He took careful aim along the barrel of his pistol and focused the sighting bead on the black windshield, driver's side.

For a moment, it looked as if the car was not going to stop, but at the last instant, the Corvette slid to a halt.

Pussy Love looked at the man standing in front of the car with the pistol trained on her. This must be Triple 'O' Seven, she thought. She checked to make sure her daughter was all right, and hitched up her already short skirt. There was a fool-proof way to deal with this man.

Pussy Love opened the door very slowly and let her long, tanned legs be the first thing that Triple 'O' Seven saw.

"Hold it!" barked Seven. "Take it real slow." With the grace of a gazelle, Pussy Love stood up from the car. She was fully aware of her sexuality and the effect it had on men. If she could get close enough to this man, she could turn the situation to her advantage.

The two of them stood staring at one another as if in some frozen tableau. The hot desert sun beat down on them both. A gust of dry wind spun Pussy Love's long blonde hair across her face. She swept it away with long delicate fingers. As her blue eyes locked onto Triple 'O' Seven's, she took a tentative step toward him. They were now only ten feet apart.

"Hold it!" gasped Triple 'O' Seven. This was not what he had expected. Standing before him was the most beautiful creature he had ever seen. He was convinced he was in love. He knew who she was, of course, from the picture he'd seen on P's desk. The pictures, however, did not do her justice. He tried to speak but no sound came out. He saw Pussy Love smile at him, her sparkling white teeth drawing his attention to her magnificent lips, which she licked quickly with the tip of her tongue. This was not a conscious sensual act, or was it? Triple 'O' Seven didn't really care. A shudder went through his entire body. Clearing his throat, he tried to speak again, and this time the words came out. "You are Pussy Love, I believe?"

"That's right," replied Pussy. She smiled, but was surprised that he knew her. "And I believe you are Triple 'O' Seven. How are you?" She took three more steps toward him before he raised the gun and held it pointing directly between her eyes. She had closed the distance between them to no more than four feet. Pussy Love believed she had him under her power from the moment he had had difficulty speaking to her. She folded her arms and smiled some more. It was only a matter of time.

Triple 'O' held the gun tightly, his hands sweating. The sun seemed hotter by the minute. He was surprised that she had known who he was. She was obviously well informed and he sensed that she was also very dangerous. But God, she was beautiful!

Her breasts strained against the flimsy material of her dress and his eyes were drawn to them. It was as if she was casting a spell over him. He quickly moved his eyes back to hers.

"Do you have a problem?" Pussy asked, a slight smile on her face.

"I think you are the one with the problem," replied Triple 'O' Seven. "After all, I'm the one with the gun."

"But I don't think you're going to use it on me. Are you?" She took another step forward. The gap between them closed. She would soon be within striking distance and kept her eyes locked on his.

"Don't be so sure. If you come one step closer, I'm afraid I will have to shoot you."

Pussy threw back her head and laughed. She laughed so much that she started to clutch her stomach. Triple 'O' Seven wondered if his fly was open. He remembered other girls who had laughed at the sight of his open fly. He was tempted to look but instead checked the zipper with his free hand. It still held. So why was she laughing? He had to be careful; it could be a ruse.

"You won't shoot me," Pussy said, struggling for breath between peals of laughter.

"I will too," retorted Triple 'O' Seven. At his reply, she fell to the ground, laughing.

"No, you won't," she stammered.

"Why?" shouted Seven. He was getting angry now and very suspicious. "What's to stop me squeezing the trigger and blowing you all over this desert?"

"Because... because...." Pussy was having trouble getting the words out. "Because...your gun. It's melting. You're all limp."

"What?" Triple 'O' Seven looked down at his gun. "God damn it!"

It was true. What at one time had been a devastating weapon was now a glommy mass of melted chocolate. The barrel had drooped downwards and twisted into a long, stretched, chewing gum-like string that reached almost to the sand. The handle of the gun was oozing from between his fingers. He opened his hand and looked at the dripping mess. There was nothing to do but laugh along with her.

"Well, I guess you're right, I'm not going to shoot you."

Pussy Love, still holding her sides and holding back laughter, moved closer to Triple 'O' and pouted her lips. She was very close to him now.

"So tell me, what dastardly deed does an English agent do in a situation like this?"

"Oh, I'm sure I can come up with something."

Pussy Love smiled at the sexual innuendo. She had him. She pouted again, and smiled. "And what do you think you can come up with?" she asked, almost purring.

"This," said Triple 'O' Seven, unleashing a quick right-hand blow to her chin. Chocolate flew everywhere. She was unconscious before her head hit the sand. She certainly was gorgeous, but he didn't trust her.

For the first time in her life, Pussy Love had underestimated her intended victim.

Chapter Eleven

CALICO

An old, full-blooded Apache Indian shuffled down the main street of Calico, or what was left of it. Gusts of dry desert wind played with the wide brim of his hat and seemed to be trying to pluck and carry away the colorful feathers stuck into the hat band. A few tumbleweeds rolled by and he swiped at them with his shovel.

The Apache Indian was known as One Finger in the Sky. He was nearly seventy-five years old. The wind and sun of the desert had tanned and leathered the old man's face, creasing it with deep lines. His dark eyes surveyed the street before him. His face was expressionless, but his sixth sense told him that he was being watched.

Following quietly behind him was his companion of many years: a mule. The mule was loaded down with turquoise, pots and pans, a bedroll and sundry other household items. He had given the mule an Indian name, Four Hooves on the

Desert Sand, which, literally translated into English, meant *Four Hooves on the Desert Sand*.

One Finger in the Sky made an annual trek into the mountains for the turquoise gemstone, which he brought back to Los Angeles and gave to the twenty-five-year-old actress he was courting. Although the girl was not an Apache, he had given her an Indian name anyway as a sign of his affection. He called her Two Legs in the Sky.

As he walked down the dusty street, he wondered what had caused all the damage. A flapping piece of roofing clanged suddenly, startling the mule. The animal's eyes widened and its nostrils flared. It seemed to also sense that they were not alone.

One Finger in the Sky's sixth sense had not let him down. He spotted the sun glinting off a piece of metal or glass high on a ridge. Someone was watching them with binoculars.

"What do you see, Mr. President?" asked Higgins. He squirmed in the saddle trying to find a more comfortable place to rest his sore behind. He was not used to riding a horse, and still wore his three-piece suit.

The President had taken the time on Air Force One to change into full western gear. He was wearing a blue satin shirt with long white fringes across the front and back and all the way down the sleeves. He wore a white Stetson because, as he explained to Higgins, all the good guys wear white hats. His outfit was complemented by matching blue satin pants, also with white fringes, and white alligator-skin cowboy boots. Higgins had arranged for horses to be waiting for them when they were dropped by helicopter just a few miles outside of Calico. The President, of course, had the only white horse and the rest of his staff had a mixture of mangy looking sorrels and blacks. The staff, like Higgins, were still dressed in their business suits and uniforms.

"I see the slimy Commie bastard. Here, look for yourself." The President handed the binoculars to Higgins.

"It looks like an old Indian prospector to me, Sir," replied Higgins.

The President grabbed the glasses back from Higgins. "Listen, Higgins, didn't American history teach you anything? Commies are masters of disguise. Now, that's a slimy Commie bastard dressed as an Indian if ever I saw one. I didn't get where I was today by not being able to recognize a slimy Commie when I see one....Is that photographer ready?"

"Yes, Sir," snapped Higgins, waving for the photographer to come forward.

The photographer spurred his horse toward them, wondering what on earth he was expected to do next. He had been sitting in the press room at the White House when two secret service agents had whisked him away. Now he found himself sitting on a mangy horse somewhere in the desert.

"Listen to me very carefully." The President doffed his hat and narrowed his eyes as he spoke to the man. "You are only going to get one chance at this. I want a series of pictures of me leading this attack. I want you to try and get me from the left because that's my best side. Is that clear?"

"Yes, Sir, Mr. President. But what are you going to attack?"

"There's a horde of filthy Commies down there who are trying to take over the world. We are going to wipe them out and off the face of this earth. At the same time, we are going to rescue the two brave secret agents named Dribble 'O' Baby and Seven Timmies."

"Sir," said Higgins. "I still only see one of the horde."

"Maybe it's a horde of one," chipped in the Secretary of Defense. He started to laugh but was silenced by a stern look from the President.

"Mark my words, we can learn from our experiences with

El Salvador and Nicaragua. They are down there all right. I reckon maybe a couple of thousand of them.''

"Two thousand of them?'' gasped Higgins. "But there's only about twenty of us, including the photographer.''

"Well, in every film I've been in, the good guys are always outnumbered. In this case, though, I have one or two tricks up my sleeve.''

"Like what?'' asked Higgins, not liking the odds at all.

"Like this.'' The President pulled his six gun from its holster and fired three shots in the air.

"You missed him, Sir, he's still standing.'' Higgins peered over the ridge to look at the Indian and the mule.

A sudden roar startled the horses as five military F-115 jets shot over them and launched a dozen or so rockets at what was left of Calico. In addition, there was the whump-whump sound of mortars being launched by the infantry, who the President had requested to dig in all around the town and wait for his signal. As the rockets obliterated the small town and flames filled the sky, the President pulled out his rifle and waved it above his head, shouting "Charge!'' Unfortunately, the barrel of the rifle hit the photographer and sent him flying unconscious from his horse.

As the President and all of his men galloped towards what was left of Calico, a mortar bomb exploded close to them ripping away their clothing and blackening their faces. Amid clearing smoke, they galloped down the main street.

"It looks like we wiped them all out. There's only one survivor. Surround him and hold him for questioning.''

One Finger in the Sky and his mule had been transfixed at the first sound of the three pistol shots. The rockets and mortars had miraculously left them unscathed. They both watched the screaming men gallop towards them. The leader in the tattered blue satin suit kept hitting people with his rifle and knocking them off their horses. He was screaming at the top of his lungs for his men to surround the Commie slime.

One Finger in the Sky looked around to see if he could see any Commie slime. There was only him and his mule standing in the street. He knew that it wasn't him, so he whirled around and hit his mule on the head with his shovel.

"How could you, Four Hooves on the Desert Sand?" The mule just stood there, stunned by the shovel.

"See that! See that!" screamed the President. "That's how those Commies treat their animals." He pulled hard on the reins and Higgins, following right behind, ran his horse into the back end of the President's. Higgins flew into the President and then thumped to the ground. "Nice riding, Higgins," praised the President. "Tie the swine up. I think a hanging would be a good way to end the day."

"Hanging's too good for a Communist mule," shouted One Finger in the Sky. "I say we barbecue him." He raised the shovel above his head, really caught up in the excitement of things.

The riders grouped behind the President cheered at the suggestion put forward by One Finger in the Sky, but they were not at all clear on what they were cheering about.

"Hold it, men!" commanded the President. He lowered the rifle barrel until it pushed against the nose of the Indian. "What's your name, scum? Higgins, write that line down. I might want to use it again."

Higgins was having a lot of difficulty in keeping up with the President's commands, especially as the President's horse had moved and was standing on one of his hands. Higgins was trying to scream but no sound came out.

"One Finger in the Sky," replied One Finger in the Sky.

"Is that your code name?"

"It's my real name," said One Finger in the Sky, suddenly realizing that he was the one they were calling a Commie, and not his mule. He wished he hadn't mentioned barbecues. This bunch of crazy white men were likely to do anything.

143

"How come you look like an Indian?" asked the President.

"I am an Indian. I'm on my way back to L.A. Look, here's my driver's licence." He fished into his jeans pocket for an old wallet as creased as his face and pulled out his licence. He handed it to Higgins, who was just managing to emerge from beneath the President's horse.

Higgins took the wallet and looked at the licence. "I'll have someone run this through the Department of Motor Vehicles." He handed the wallet to Gregory, Secretary of the Navy, who rode off towards the ridge.

The President looked at One Finger in the Sky suspiciously. He still kept the rifle barrel pointed right at his nose. "Well, we can check this out pretty quick. If you are a real Indian, who was the star of the film *Little Big Man*?"

"Dustin Hoffman," replied One Finger in the Sky.

"Do you know who I am?" asked the President, relaxing a little.

"Dustin Hoffman?" said One Finger in the Sky, tentatively.

It was the wrong thing to say. The President pulled back the hammer on the rifle. One Finger in the Sky thought he was on his way to the happy hunting ground, but now it looked as if he'd be shot before he got anywhere *near* L.A. The eyes of the President sparkled with excitement. The mortar shell that had exploded close to the riders had left a ring of soot around the President's eyes which made it appear like he was wearing a mask. Could this be...?

One Finger in the Sky watched the knuckles of the hand holding the rifle whiten as pressure was applied to the trigger.

"Sir! Sir!" shouted Gregory, galloping up to the riders. "He checks out. He is who he says he is."

The President almost looked disappointed as he pulled back the rifle from the Indian's nose. "An Indian, huh? What are you doing here?"

"I'm on my way to L.A. to see my girlfriend, and I always make a point of stopping here to see Timmy Baby."

"That's one of the agents," said Higgins excitedly.

"Do you know where he is?" asked the President.

One Finger in the Sky suddenly found that these men were hanging onto his every word. He used the opportunity to slip into his best 'Indian language'.

"They have taken great silver bird that leaves large white trails in the sky...."

"What's he saying, Sir?" said Higgins.

"They caught a seagull?" said the President.

"They travel west over great water...."

"They've gone water skiing, Higgins. What are they doing going water skiing?"

One Finger in the Sky hesitated before continuing. He wondered if something was drastically wrong with his best Indian language. He tried again. "They have gone to the land of great pot."

"They have dysentery!" exclaimed the President.

One Finger in the Sky gave up. He handed a note to Higgins, who read it out loud. Timmy Baby had pinned the note to his door for One Finger in the Sky.

"Mr. President," said Higgins, "I think what the Indian is trying to say is that the two agents left for Hawaii on Western Airlines Flight 109."

The President turned around in his saddle and addressed his men. "It looks like we have just missed the two agents, Seven Triple Babies and Baby 'O' Tummy. In all likelihood they are still in trouble. It is still our job to save them, and they may have the answer to what in God's name is happening. We will have a five minute rest and then we ride for Hawaii. One Finger in the Sky, from now on you will be my tracker. It will look good in the newspapers to have a member of a minority gainfully employed. Do you have any pork and beans for my men?"

145

"Just some dead squirrels," answered One Finger in the Sky.

"Good," said the President. "Make up a bunch of squirrel sandwiches, with jam. I'll be on the ridge." With that, the President spurred his horse, pulled on the reins and rode off. Unfortunately, he didn't see Higgins, who was knocked to the ground by the President's horse.

One Finger in the Sky moved toward Higgins and helped him stand. "Who was that masked man?"

"That," replied Higgins, "is the fucking President of the United States."

One Finger in the Sky looked up to the crest of the ridge. For the benefit of his men below, the President pulled the horse's reins sharply, raising it up onto its hind legs.

"Oh, wow!" said One Finger in the Sky. They all looked on as the President slid off the rear end of the animal and landed in a cloud of dust.

Chapter Twelve

HAWAII

"She sure is beautiful," said Timmy Baby, looking at the unconscious Pussy Love who lay sleeping with her daughter. "She should be out for another few hours. Do you think that's enough time to reach their base?"

"I don't know," replied Triple 'O' Seven. "I just hope the information she gave us was correct."

As soon as Triple 'O' Seven had taken the unconscious Pussy Love back to Timmy Baby's place with her daughter, Timmy had administered sodium pentathol, a truth drug, into Pussy's blood stream and slowly the information had been released from those gorgeous lips. It had not taken Timmy and Triple 'O' Seven long to piece together the connection between the dead C.I.A. agent and the equally dead Molokai bar owner. They had made a quick call to the Hawaii State Department of Wildlife and Preservation and found out that there were five such bird sanctuaries, but only

147

one which both avid bird watchers had been granted permission to visit: Manana Island.

One more call by Timmy and they were all on their way to Hawaii. They were now at the British Embassy on Makawaii Street opposite the main post office building in Waikiki.

The Embassy staff were surprised to see the four of them standing at the front door, one of them an unconscious woman, and one a small child.

They did not explain anything to the staff except that they were working with the British government on a top secret mission. They had provided the Ambassador with the internal top secret code which afforded them immediate access and co-operation. They were housed in clean, small rooms that smelled of fresh flowers.

The Ambassador looked as one would envisage a diplomat. He was in his early sixties, very distinguished, with a shock of grey hair outlining a deeply tanned face. His accent was almost contrived, with a heavy Oxford flavour.

"I say, chaps," said the Ambassador, "isn't there anything you can tell me. I mean, all this cloak and dagger stuff just doesn't happen all that often here. I mean, it would be positively awful if I, as it were, positively screwed up the whole bailiwick, so to speak."

"All we can tell you, Ambassador, is that her name is Pussy," said Triple 'O' Seven.

"I beg your pardon?"

"Pussy," echoed Timmy, "and her little girl is called Kitty."

"It's going to be awfully embarrassing having Pussy in the Embassy. I mean, what if my polo friends find out I've got Pussy here?"

"You must not let it leak," said Timmy emphatically.

"I beg your pardon?"

"You must not let anyone know she is here," said Triple 'O' Seven. "I want a guard on the door at all times." He pulled the light sheet up under the chins of Pussy Love and her daughter. "For security reasons, you cannot even let London know she is here. I think we have a mole in our organization."

"A mole?"

"Yes, someone in London must be working against us. It's the only way they could have known the exact time I was arriving in Los Angeles. They knew Timmy lived in Calico and set a trap for us. This woman could be a link to both the mole and the mastermind behind three terrible murders and God knows what else. It's imperative that no one knows she is here."

"Roger," said the Ambassador.

"What?"

"Roger. A—OK. Over and out. Message understood." The Ambassador stood to attention and gave a very smart British army salute. "You can depend on me."

"Good," said Timmy Baby. "Now perhaps you can show us to the Embassy supply room. Triple 'O' told me that someone called U said you might have a supply of weapons and gadgets here that we can use."

As they left, they made sure the guard was reminded not to let anyone near the occupants of the room. The Ambassador led the way through the corridors of the large Baronial mansion that served as the Embassy. The staff numbered no more than ten at any one time, but even so it was unusually empty. However, it was very rare that the Embassy had to deal with anything other than tourists' stolen passports.

Under the influence of the truth serum, Pussy Love had rambled on about making contact with an 'Agent Irma' in Hawaii. She had also mentioned the leper colony at Molokai. At first it had not made much sense to the two agents, but the phone call to the Department of Wildlife and Preservation had shed some light. There was something going on at

149

Manana Island.

Triple 'O' Seven was sure that someone back in London was feeding information as to their whereabouts, and he deemed it prudent not to inform London of his subsequent move to Hawaii. He had called U directly, sworn him to secrecy, and inquired about what stock of weapons were kept at the Embassy.

"Here we go, chaps." The Ambassador took out a key and opened the small door that led into one of the basement rooms. "I'm afraid we haven't had much call to use this stuff. Why don't you see if there's anything you can use, and just make yourself at home." He checked the time. "Well, if you will excuse me, I have to watch my son play that infernal game of American football."

The Ambassador left with a wave of his hand.

"Nice chap," Seven said, turning to Timmy Baby, but Timmy Baby was already losing himself in all the crates and boxes that lay around the room.

"Find anything?"

"Well, I think we might just be in luck. Have you ever flown a helicopter before?" Timmy asked.

"No."

"Well, you are about to experience your first helicopter flight. Come on, give me a hand, grab one of these."

Triple 'O' grabbed one of the boxes that Timmy dragged out. They were long and weighed about fifty pounds each.

"These are helicopters?" said Triple 'O' Seven, a certain amount of disbelief in his voice.

"Yes. Miniature one-man helicopters that you strap on your back. They are powered by propane and have six rockets for assault and attack purposes. They travel at about one hundred miles per hour and have a range of some five hundred miles."

"How the hell do you know so much about these things?"

"It says so on the box," Timmy replied, hoisting one of

150

them onto his shoulder. They took the helicopters out onto the front lawn of the Embassy and began to assemble them.

The small helicopters were powered by two micro-sized jet engines on the end of the rotor arms. The engines were fueled by a pressurized propane tank made of a special light alloy which was strapped onto the pilot's back. The attack rockets were in vertical racks that fit snugly down each side of the body.

"Whatever you do, don't touch the firing button on the left hand control," said Timmy Baby, pointing to the attack rockets. "And remember, this machine is one hundred percent throttle-able. Let's go. If you get nervous, just take down the throttle." Timmy put on his helmet and took off. It looked easy.

With a roar, the small jet engines started to turn the rotor above Triple 'O' Seven's head. It made a swishing sound and suddenly Triple 'O' Seven was airborne. He swung backwards and forwards out of control and quickly pulled back on the throttle. Timmy Baby swung towards him in a graceful arc. "Take it easy and try to lean forward a little," he shouted over the noise.

Seven readjusted the helmet which made him look like a grotesque creature from outer space and tried the throttle again. This time he did not have any control problems.

They made their way out over the Waikiki beach.

"Do you notice anything strange?" asked Triple 'O' Seven, into his radio mike.

"Yes, I do. I was just going to ask you the same thing. There's hardly anyone on the beach and yet it's a great day. I wonder what's happening. Let's head inland and go over the mountains. We should be at Manana Island in about twenty minutes."

They turned toward Diamond Head.

As they skimmed over the houses and shopping centres, there seemed to be an unusual lack of activity below them.

The streets, in particular, were practically empty, and every so often they would spot a car that had apparently just stopped in the middle of the road, immobile except for a slight rocking of the vehicle on its chassis.

Timmy Baby and Triple 'O' flew over a small rise and abruptly found themselves not too far above a football game. To his left, Triple 'O' Seven could see the kick-off. It was a high, soaring kick. What a beauty, he thought, but suddenly Triple 'O' realized the football was heading straight for him. He tried to veer out of its way but he was too late. The ball hit the firing button and all six attack rockets hurtled towards the playing field. A huge eruption of smoke and earth rocked the two of them, carrying them away from the field. They were almost two miles away before they could control their helicopters.

"What the hell happened?" shouted Timmy Baby.

"I got hit with a football," explained Triple 'O' Seven. "It's an incredibly violent game, isn't it?"

The meagre crowd of spectators sat staring dumbfounded at where the home team had once been getting ready to receive the kick-off. There was nothing but a gaping hole. Luck was with the players, though. Because of padding and helmets, they were only stunned, bruised and deafened. Some of them had gone on unscheduled flights and landed in the swimming pools, barbecues, and gardens of the homes surrounding the field.

•

Manana Island, also known to the locals as Rabbit Island, was like a jewel within nature's already beautiful setting. The clear blue of the ocean surrounded it and the surf beat at its shores. As Triple 'O' Seven and Timmy Baby approached the island, the birds objected strongly to the whine of the jet engines and shrilled their disapproval. The noise was deafening as thousands of birds rose from the rocky terrain and circled the unwelcome visitors.

"I don't see anything here at all," Timmy shouted.

"Let's fly over the island before landing, maybe we can spot something," replied Triple 'O'.

Manana Island is not very large, perhaps three quarters of a mile long at most, and it didn't take long to fly over it.

"I still don't see anything," said Timmy.

"Neither do I," said Triple 'O' Seven, wheeling around to make another pass over the island. "But everything points to here. There must be something. Wait a minute. Look! Over there." He pointed to a small rise on the eastern tip of the island.

"I see it," said Timmy, and they both whirred towards the rise.

Seven had seen the faintest wisp of what looked like steam. Another puff, and then it was gone. But not before they had zeroed in on where it had come from. They set down close to a pile of rocks.

"Bingo," said Triple 'O' Seven as he unbuckled his helicopter and ran towards the rocks. "A ventilation shaft."

Cleverly hidden by the pile of rocks was what looked like a huge ventilation shaft. The air coming out of the shaft was cold and stale. Triple 'O' Seven and Timmy looked down but could see nothing, and heard only the very faint whirr of an air conditioning plant.

"Well, I wonder what we have here," said Timmy.

"Can you hear anything else?" Triple 'O' Seven asked, hoping that Timmy's refined senses would once again prove useful.

Timmy put his ear to the metal but the screeching of the birds above made it impossible for Timmy to pick out any other sounds. He looked up.

"Maybe Big Bird has a nest down there," said Timmy.

"I think we should have a look, don't you?"

They moved the flat rock-strewn grill that covered the shaft and worked their way into the opening. The only way to get down was to use an old rock-climbing trick that mountain climbers called 'chimney walking'. It was a safe and easy way to descend, feet against one wall and back against the other.

Timmy Baby went first, quickly followed by Triple 'O' Seven.

"Will you get your foot off my hand?" whispered Timmy Baby.

Even though he spoke in a whisper, the sound was amplified into a shout by the confined space.

"Sorry, I was just taking another one of these pills that U gave me. I didn't notice anything last time I took one, maybe I should take two this time." Triple 'O' Seven popped two of the pills into his mouth, closed the capsule and placed it back in his pocket. Just like last time, he suddenly felt thirsty.

"I think you're turning orange," said Timmy.

"Don't make jokes like that. These pills are supposed to make me a mean, fighting machine, according to U."

They both made their way down the shaft which got darker and darker as they descended. The noise became louder, almost to the point of being painful.

At last they reached a horizontal portion of the ducting. They chose to go to the right and had crawled perhaps fifty feet when they came to a large grill they could see through. They were up high, maybe sixty feet above a huge cavern. The view was perfect.

"Christ! What the hell is going on here?" whispered Timmy.

"I don't know, it looks like a factory of some sort."

Far below them, white-coated workers busied themselves at what looked like a production line for aerosol spray cans. The sparkling clean machinery whirred and spun as it processed the containers.

"They are all wearing masks, whatever is in those cans must be dangerous or toxic," Timmy whispered.

"We had better get a closer look and find out what's going on. I don't like this at all," said Triple 'O'. "And make a note of where those guards are, it looks like there are about twenty of them." He scanned the area for more but could see none, although he reasoned there was bound to be more somewhere.

They moved along the air conditioning duct trying not to make any noise. As they left the factory area, the ducting again became dark, but ahead of them light came through another grill. They reached it and looked down into another cavern.

"I don't believe it. A mini-submarine base."

"What a set-up. That's how this place remains so secret," said Triple 'O'.

More heavily armed guards patrolled the dock where three mini-subs were moored. They were painted bright yellow and looked like smaller versions of large nuclear-powered subs. A claxon horn rang and the guards went into formation.

"Look," said Triple 'O' Seven. "Down there."

The claxon horn stopped and they could see a group of people walking towards one of the submarines.

"They must be the brass. Look how the hands salute them," said Timmy.

"What a weird looking bunch," said Triple 'O', as he watched them. The obvious leader was a huge black man with the hands of a white man. He was carrying a white cat. As he barked out orders, the others—an albino, a Chinese fat man, and an old woman—listened to him. From this vantage point, Triple 'O' Seven and Timmy Baby could hear his booming voice.

"We must all go to the base in Florida immediately," the black man was saying. "Phase One is proceeding even as I speak, with excellent results. We will be ready to execute Phase Two within six hours of our arrival. We cannot afford any delays.''

"Don't you want us to stay here and supervise the operation from this end, Bloh Jobb?'' the albino asked.

"No, Dr. Maybe,'' the leader replied, "I want you and Dr. Yes with me when we put this plan into its final phase. We have a problem at the British Embassy in Oahu. Miss Klogg has been informed that the two agents somehow managed to escape our trap in Calico and have captured Pussy Love. They have obviously obtained information from her somehow, and she has led them to Oahu.

"I have ordered that the Embassy staff be terminated immediately and Pussy Love be brought to me in the Marquesas Keys. We need to find out how much she told them. Fortunately, she knew very little, and I expect to have these agents killed along with the Embassy staff before they put two and two together.''

In the air duct, Triple 'O' Seven began to crawl forward as fast as he could, silently cursing the enormous man as he went. Timmy took a last look and followed.

"They will never find us here,'' Dr. Yes was saying to his brother.

Bloh Jobb took Irma aside. "I have an uncomfortable feeling these agents could be dangerous if allowed to live. We should hear of their extermination by the time we get to our base in Florida.'' With that, Bloh Jobb led the group onto the deck of the mini-sub and into the hatch which a guard held open for them. The claxon horn blared again and the sub started to slip under the water.

Triple 'O' Seven silently damned the Ambassador. He must have ignored his instructions not to inform London. Now the Embassy was to be wiped out. They had to find out what was going on here and get to the Embassy as fast as they could. Then they had to get to Florida.

They made their way along the duct until they came to a grill which opened up into the huge engine room that drove the air conditioners. The noise was almost deafening. Timmy Baby kicked out the grill and they jumped to the concrete floor. Opening the door, they looked quietly into the corridor and saw two guards approaching. When the guards were almost opposite the door, they sprang out, decked them both with quick blows to the throat, and dragged the limp bodies back into the engine room.

In a few moments, Triple 'O' Seven and Timmy emerged wearing the uniforms of the unconscious guards. A face mask with an air filtering device dangled from each of their belts.

"Not a bad fit," shouted Triple 'O' Seven, as he held the sub-machine-gun and cocked it. Timmy did the same, and they walked back towards the large cavern that held the factory. Passing quickly through the mini-submarine base, they made mental notes of all strategic elements necessary for an escape. If they were to get out of here, this would be the way they would have to go.

They trotted down another short corridor which opened up to the vast subterranean chamber and the factory. The machinery hummed and clicked as it churned out the small, shiny cans by the thousands. They walked slowly around the sparkling clean premises.

"What do you make of it?" asked Timmy.

"I don't know, they just look like spray cans. I think if we get closer, we should wear these masks. Let's make our way over to where they're putting on the labels. Geez, I'm thirsty. Those damn pills of U's are driving me crazy."

"Stop opening and closing your mouth, you're starting to look like a goldfish," said Timmy, pushing his mask over his face.

They made their way over to where the equipment slapped brightly coloured labels onto the aerosol cans. Triple 'O'

Seven picked out one of the spray cans from the endless stream that trundled by on the steel conveyor system.

"Good God!" he exclaimed, his eyes widening with surprise, behind his mask.

Timmy sucked in his breath when he saw the label. "I don't believe it!" said Timmy.

"It's underarm deodorant!" said Triple 'O'. "And look at this:

> *Help a Girl Guide Today*
> *Use This Effective Spray*

Quite a slogan."

"Holy shit!" said Timmy. "Maybe the Girl Guides own this place. Maybe they are working with this Bloh Jobb character in some plot or something."

"Maybe it's the Boy Scouts," countered Triple 'O' Seven. "Or maybe Girl Guides just smell a lot."

Their discussion was interrupted by the sound of a loud voice. "Hey! What are you doing?"

Triple 'O' Seven whirled around to find a guard standing right behind them, pointing his gun.

Seven still held the spray can and now he pressed the nozzle, sending a fine spray into the guard's eyes. The guard screamed, rubbed his eyes and fell backwards into the labelling machine. The label punch, a hydraulic-driven steel arm, cut the man's scream short as it passed through his chest, killing him instantly. The machine tried to keep stamping labels, but with the guard's body fouling up the works, the cans all backed up and started to fall to the floor, setting off the alarm.

"Let's get out of here!" yelled Triple 'O' Seven.

Timmy let go a short burst from his sub-machine-gun as guards started to raise their own weapons. Timmy also hit some electrical conduit that ran along one of the far walls of the cavern, filling the room with sparks and smoke. The white-coated workers, unarmed, ducked for cover or ran for safety. Amid all the confusion, Triple 'O' Seven and Timmy Baby mingled with the other guards. With their stolen uniforms and masks, they were virtually indistinguishable, and they soon made their way to the corridor leading to the mini-sub docking bays. The factory was in pandemonium as they left. Bullets were still being sprayed recklessly by nervous guards, and they could hear the screams of the white-coated workers. There was an explosion and Triple 'O' Seven and Timmy were thrown to the floor. They gasped for air as a tremendous wave of heat filled the corridor.

A group of guards from the submarine room ran towards them, guns at the ready. Timmy and Triple 'O' let a burst of fire loose from their weapons. Several of the guards dropped, and others took cover in another corridor.

"Keep firing and run for it," yelled Triple 'O' Seven, jumping up and leading the way.

"I wish I had a joint right now," Timmy yelled back.

With weapons spitting death, they charged past the guards' position. They ran through a set of doors and entered the submarine cave.

"Quick, let's take the yellow one. I'll cover, you untie the ropes," said Timmy, and he let another hail of bullets go towards the door. Two more guards fell, but some made it through and opened fire. The bullets pinged off the metal body of the mini-sub as Triple 'O' Seven cast away the mooring ropes.

"You forgot that these things are *both* yellow," he shouted.

"I knew I should have smoked a joint," replied Timmy. He stood up from behind a wooden crate and let another salvo of shells go towards the guards.

"Let's go." Triple 'O' Seven lifted up the hatch and dropped down into the mini-sub.

Firing as he ran, Timmy jumped for the conning tower, dived inside, and closed the hatch after him. He turned the hatch lock and dropped into the small interior of the sub. The noise of shells hitting the outside of the hull reverberated throughout the small craft.

"Do you know how to drive one of these things?" Timmy asked.

Triple 'O' Seven sat down in front of what was obviously the control centre of the sub. The myriad of dials and gauges stared up at him, looking something like the control panels of an airplane. "No problem." He twisted a key and the submarine started to throb as the screws turned. He pulled levers and twisted dials. The submarine lurched forward and struck the dock. "Ooops." It then twisted around in its berth and hit the other submarine. "Look in the periscope and see what you can see."

Timmy had second-guessed him and was already raising it. He looked through the eyepiece and saw that the cavern was full of people trying to escape the inferno of the exploding underarm deodorant factory. A face suddenly popped up at the other end of the periscope. Some of the guards were trying to open up the hatch.

"Take her down quick. They're trying to get into this bucket."

"I wish I could. Oh! Hold it! I think this is the one." Triple 'O' pulled down a lever until a small red arrow pointed at the letter 'D'. A roar of bubbles escaped from the submarine and sent vibrations through the craft. "Hold on!" shouted Triple 'O' Seven.

The sub quickly sank below the surface of the water. There were a number of guards on the sub who clung desperately, as if they could somehow hold the submarine above the water, but finally their lungs cried for oxygen. They swam to the surface to meet their fate.

The submarine hummed as it made its way through the tunnel leading from the cavern to the open sea. After about two minutes, they noticed a change in the water.

"We must be in the open water now," said Timmy, peering through the periscope. "The water here is much lighter, so there must be sky above. Take her up, we can't be that far from the beach."

As the periscope of the submarine broke surface, Timmy noticed two large helicopters heading for the island. "I wonder who they are?"

"Who?"

"There's two helicopters heading for the island."

There was a sudden lurch as the submarine hit the beach at Kailua. A startled windsurfer hit the conning tower of the submarine and fell into the shallow water. He was even more shocked when two men carrying sub-machine-guns popped out of the sub.

"Don't shoot! Don't shoot! It wasn't my fault, I promise not to hit your submarine again!"

"What's he saying?" Triple 'O' Seven asked.

"Beats me. Let's go. We have to get to the Embassy."

Chapter Thirteen

MANANA ISLAND

As the President approached Manana Island in Chopper One, the official helicopter of the President of the United States, the birds, shrieking and wheeling from the noises and rumbles they could feel beneath them, were even further angered at having their air space violated for the second time that day.

"This reminds me of Hickock's film, *The Birds*," said the President to Higgins. "Birds are vile creatures, Higgins. They carry all sorts of disgusting diseases."

"Wasn't Hickock in the film, *Gun Fight at the O.K. Corral?*" asked Higgins, wearily. He was getting tired of correcting the President.

"They don't have birds in westerns, Higgins." The President was about to explain exactly why they did not have birds in westerns when the helicopter set down. "One Finger in the Sky, get your ass down here."

The President jumped from the helicopter and his alligator cowboy boots promptly sank into about a foot of bird droppings. One Finger In The Sky jumped down beside him. "See any signs of life?" asked the President.

One Finger In The Sky slipped into his Indian role.

"Oh, Great White Chief of white men, White Chief who flies in great metal bird. I *do* see signs of life."

"What do you see, my red brother?" said the President, slipping into his role of the Great White Chief. "Write that line down, Higgins. I might want to use that again someday when I'm talking to the Commies at the United Nations."

"Great White Chief, I see about one foot of bird shit over the whole island."

The President slapped One Finger In The Sky on the back. "Well done, my fine feathered friend."

"What does it mean?" asked Higgins.

The rest of the men debarked from Chopper One and unloaded the horses from the other helicopter. The President took the reins of his horse and climbed into the saddle. It was time for some inspiring words.

"Men," began the President, "the two agents were seen heading for this island. We have got to find those agents. Now, One Finger In The Sky here, has pointed out that there is one foot of bird shit over the entire island."

"But what does it mean?" interrupted Higgins.

"It means that we are dealing with a very big bird."

The President's men looked at one another and said nothing. They climbed onto their horses and waited for the inevitable order to ride.

The President was about to so order when he heard a rumble from deep within the bowels of the island. "Higgins. What's that noise?"

"Sounds like a rumble from deep within the bowels of the island, sir."

"I know it sounds like a rumble from deep within the

164

bowels of the island, but what's causing it?'' He looked to One Finger In The Sky for an explanation.

"Oh Great White Chief, I fear the gods of the Bird Island are angry. I fear the big bird is about to shit on us from below.''

The horses became skittish and started to panic as the ground began to shake beneath their hooves.

"What's he saying, Higgins?''

"I think he's saying that the island is about to explode, Sir.'' Higgins was having a difficult time holding onto his horse.

"Ridiculous. That would never happen in the United States. It's against the law to explode a bird sanctuary without a permit.''

Cliff Stripper, a warden with the State of Hawaii's Department of Wildlife and Preservation, slammed on the brakes of his Toyota Jeep. He grabbed his binoculars and looked across the water at Manana Island. He was right, he had seen a puff of smoke. As he focused the glasses, he also saw the two large helicopters and about a dozen men riding horses. "What the hell are they doing, don't they know that that island is the home of Bulwer's Petrel, one of the world's rarest birds?''

He was about to pick up the mobile telephone and report the presence of the intruders when a blinding flash and a huge roar obliterated the island from view.

•

The door of the the Embassy crashed open under the foot of Triple 'O' Seven. Holding his foot, he hopped inside the cool, white foyer and limped for the bedroom where they had left Pussy Love and her daughter peacefully sleeping. Timmy

165

Baby kept close to him, ready to give covering fire if he needed it.

In grim silence Triple 'O' Seven and Timmy went through the Embassy. No one had been spared. Pussy Love and her daughter were nowhere to be seen. The Ambassador was sprawled on the plush carpet in front of them. His throat had been cut.

"God-damn it! The stupid fool," said Triple 'O' angrily. "I told him not to tell anyone, but he must have checked us with the London Embassy and they probably checked with H.Q. It will be a pleasure to deal with our little spy."

"What do we do now?"

"We go to Florida. What did that man....what's his name?"

"Bloh Jobb."

"That's right. He said that he was going to the Marquesas Keys. Where is that?"

"Maybe that will tell us."

They walked over to a large wall map of North America and studied Florida.

"Here it is," said Triple 'O' Seven, grabbing a pencil and circling the tiny island at the very end of an archipelago some distance from the tip of Florida. The nearest airport was at Key West. From there, they would need a boat. "Remember what that fiend Bloh Jobb said. The final phase of their plan is ready to be put into operation within the next six hours. And this tiny island is where we will find out what's going on."

Timmy looked at his watch. "They've got quite a start on us. By my watch, we only have a shade over five hours left."

"We can't waste any more time. Let's go."

•

The windsurfer was relaxing from the shock of hitting the mini-sub earlier in the day. His thin board and bright red sail

166

skimmed over the waves. All of a sudden a man riding a white horse emerged from the water ten yards in front and fired a warning shot that nearly pierced the windsurfer's ear. He crashed to the water and vowed to quit smoking Hawaiian grass.

"God-damn hippies!" shouted the President, surging past the submerged windsurfer. "Higgins. Higgins! I want you to get me the name of whoever it was that blew up that bird sanctuary without a permit."

"Yes, sir," replied Higgins dejectedly. Some of his hair had blown away in the explosion and his face was blackened. The rest of the President's men followed close behind, clinging for dear life to the soaking manes of their mounts. Their wet clothes were tattered and hanging in strips from their bodies. They were scratched, bruised and shaken.

They rode out of the crashing surf and up onto the white sand, following dutifully behind their leader. Most of them wanted to go home, but nothing was said. They were resigned to following the President, and all of them knew it was far from over.

One Finger In The Sky rode up beside the President. His mule, Four Hooves in the Desert Sand, was also wondering what was going to happen next. In the last little while, he had been hit with a shovel, bombed, strafed, flown all over the place in a helicopter, and blown up. He was looking at the President's horse with slightly shell-shocked eyes.

"Kemo Sabby, I ...."

"What the hell are you talking about?" snapped the President.

"That's what the Lone Ranger's Indian friend used to say," offered Higgins.

"Oh, really. The Lone Ranger, huh. Well spit it out, my faithful companion." The President smiled his best camera smile. He was back into the role of the brave cowboy.

"Kemo Sabby, maybe we should check at the British

Embassy. Maybe tracks will tell us something.''

"Of course. Great idea. Men, we ride. Yooo!'' With a flourish of his arm, the President led his men in a full gallop for Waikiki.

●

High above the blue Gulf of Mexico, Bloh Jobb's private jet hurtled toward Key West. Time was now of the utmost importance. Unaware of what had happened back at the island production facility, he was relaxing in his luxurious private cabin and enjoying a drink. The cabin was located at the back of the plane and was very spacious and roomy. Bloh Jobb was sitting behind a huge desk. His cat was on his lap and he was working with a calculator, checking his figures for the destruction of the world economy. Behind him was a richly appointed bathroom and along one side of the cabin was a large king-sized bed covered with a deep wool pile bedspread. A thick white carpet spread across the floor. The roof of the cabin was all mirrors; Bloh Jobb occasionally liked to watch himself make love to a beautiful woman.

There was a knock on the door.

"Come,'' said Bloh Jobb, without looking up from the maze of figures shooting across the face of his calculator.

Irma Klogg entered the cabin and closed the door behind her. She leaned up against it in what she thought was a seductive pose, a shoulder bag slung over her arm. It was time to give herself to this man. Jobb's aura of power and masculinity sent shivers through her body, filling her with desire.

"Yes,'' Bloh Jobb said, still not looking up at her.

"I just thought you might like a little company,'' Irma said, as seductively as she could. However, the effect was lost on Bloh Jobb, who remained intent on his calculations.

"Put my cat out, would you?'' Bloh Jobb held up the

white cat with his free hand, still without looking up from the calculator. The cat hissed at Irma as she approached.

Irma smiled and pressed down on the heel of her heavy shoes. The poisonous metal blade popped out from the toe cap with the faintest of clicks. She took the hissing cat by the scruff of the neck and held it out in front of her. "Of course I'll put your cat out. It will be a pleasure." As she walked to the door, she murmured, "Permanently." Irma opened the door and dropped the cat, at the same time aiming a kick at the animal. It expired noiselessly on the end of her shoe. She shook her foot and the dead animal dropped to the floor. She gave it another kick and it slid underneath one of the airplane seats, coming to rest as if it was asleep.

She stepped back into the room and retracted the steel blade in her shoe. Droplets of blood fell to the white carpet and started to spread in ever-widening circles. Irma smiled, happy that the cat was gone. She had been wanting to do that from the first time she had met this man. The cat had always hated her. "I'd just like to use your bathroom to freshen up."

Bloh Jobb grunted. He was totally absorbed.

Irma slipped into the bathroom and opened up the shoulder bag. It was time to seduce this magnificent man. She was convinced that all men liked dominant women, and she was going to provide him with the ultimate in dominant pleasure.

Bloh Jobb sat back in his chair and chuckled to himself. Very soon now he would be the most powerful man in the world. His hideous scheme had worked so very, very well. He was about to take a congratulatory sip of his Scotch when the long cracking tail of a whip wound itself around his neck. His glass flew against the wall of the cabin and he fell backwards from his chair. A black high-heeled boot pressed down on his upper chest. Off his guard and completely surprised, Bloh Jobb looked up at Irma. He stared with shock and then started to smile, which quickly became a chuckle and turned into booming laughter.

Irma had changed into a negligee that revealed her pendulous breasts. She was wearing panties, a black garter belt, mesh stockings and a black hooded mask. It was the black mask that made Bloh Jobb laugh.

Irma pressed harder with her high heel. There was a grimace of pain from Bloh Jobb and he stopped laughing. A shiny steel blade was sticking out from the toe of her boot, a hair's breadth away from the soft flesh of his throat. Irma pushed very slightly.

"Whatever you do, don't move, my darling," said Irma, licking her lips. "The slightest break in your skin and the poison on these blades will kill you within five seconds."

"My darling?" said the incredulous Bloh Jobb. "Oh my God! I'm going to be raped."

"I want you to ask me to rape you. And don't forget to call me 'Mistress Irma' when you speak to me." She pulled on the whip that was still wrapped around his neck.

Bloh Jobb could almost feel the pressure of the steel blade against his neck. This crazy woman had him. Him, a man many times her strength, at her mercy. One slip, and it would be all over. He had to buy some time. He was furious. Everything he had worked for...all his plans had gone *so well*, and now this crazy, horny, old woman would ruin it all. He needed some time.

"Yes, Mistress Irma," he croaked.

"That's better, you slut. You need to be taught a lesson, don't you?"

"Yes, Mistress Irma."

"What are you?"

"I'm a slut, Mistress Irma."

Bloh Jobb's temper was rising. Never had he been so humiliated. He fought to get himself under control. He looked up into the grinning face of Irma.

170

Irma was in seventh heaven. Here at last was her moment, and she savoured every precious second of it. She licked her lips and smiled again.

"Get your pants off, slut. Slowly does it." Irma pulled on the whip again. Bloh Jobb was now getting to the point of blacking out. He struggled with the belt of his pants and slid them down as far as he could. In her other hand Irma had a short riding crop. She slapped Bloh Jobb across the thighs. He winced but dare not move for fear that Irma's deadly blade would go into his neck.

He would kill this woman. He would snap her neck as many times as he could. He would break every bone in her body. All he needed was one split second.

Irma licked her lips again. She had seen Bloh Jobb's manhood. "Oh, my. Oh, my," she said, dizzy with pleasure. Here was the most powerful man in the world completely at her mercy. Now it was time to make him perform.

"You are going to do everything I say, Bloh Jobb," she said, with a horrible theatrical laugh. She pulled the whip again and Bloh Jobb almost lost consciousness from lack of oxygen. "I know that you are planning to double-cross General Bretzky, and he wouldn't like that if he knew, would he?" She pulled the whip again.

"No, Mistress Irma," choked Bloh Jobb.

"I also know that you plan to get rid of the twins at the first possible moment. My guess is that it will be about five minutes after you put your plan into effect. Right?"

"Yes, Mistress Irma."

"Louder! You slut!" She gave Bloh Jobb a stinging blow to the groin with the riding crop. He wiggled under the carefully placed stroke.

"Yes, Mistress Irma," Bloh Jobb gritted.

"That's better, darling. Now, if I was to tell General Bretzky and the twins what you had planned, it would cause untold problems for you, wouldn't it? However, if you want

171

everything to go as smooth as silk, all you have to do is, how do you say, in English?"

"Fuck you!" choked Bloh Jobb.

"Yes, that's it exactly. Fill me with your manhood." She prodded him with the riding crop. "Now then, what do you say?"

Bloh Jobb could not believe for one minute that this was happening to him. He couldn't believe that Irma was doing this to him. Klogg, of all people. He was being raped. Raped! He needed time. He must play along with her. He gave the slightest nod, fearful that at any moment the tip of the poisoned blade would enter his throat.

Irma let out a throaty laugh. "Well, now. Saying is one thing, doing is another. Let's just see how big you are. Let's get you ready for sex. I want the ultimate Bloh Jobb." She toyed with his flaccid penis. "Come on, Jobb, you can do better than that, I'm sure."

Through all the frustration, humiliation and anger, Bloh Jobb found, to his surprise, that under the administration of the riding crop, his manhood responded.

"Ah! What a sight. But you can still do better. There. Now we are getting somewhere." Irma's attention was now riveted on the sight of his erection, her lips quivering in anticipation.

For a split second, the fraction of time that Bloh Jobb needed, he felt the pressure ease on his chest. With a quick blow to her ankle, he swept the poisoned blade away from his throat and sprang to his feet. He teetered, slightly off balance, because his pants were around his ankles. In spite of this, he ripped the whip away from her grasp and began to unwind it from around his neck.

"So. You bitch. Do you think anyone could ever get away with doing something like that to me? Do you think that I give a shit whether the great General Bretzky ever finds out what I plan to do? Or if the twins are told what they already

172

suspect? Don't you understand that it's too late for them to change the course of their fates and the fates of millions of other people? Can't you get it through that ugly head of yours that I will be master of this universe and that anyone who dares interfere with that plan will die, just as you are about to die?''

Irma had shaken herself from her sexual excitement and now knew that the end was near. She pressed down on her other heel and a second poisonous blade sprang from the tip of the high heeled boot. There was still a chance that she could scratch him when he attacked her. Five seconds after that he would be dead. But she had to hit him with the blades of her shoes first, or it was all over.

She leapt at him with her feet high in the air. Bloh Jobb moved easily away, but twisted his ankle on his Scotch glass and fell to the floor.

She aimed another kick at his head. In the nick of time, he moved away. The blade parted his hair and sank into the wooden desk. A sudden thought came to Irma. She was certainly trusted by General Bretzky, and if she could kill Bloh Jobb, maybe she could take his place. She had to try. The only problem was that the blade of her shoe was stuck in the desk.

In the moments that it took to free herself, Bloh Jobb had managed to stand and pull his pants up. He was now ready to kill. One look into his eyes, and Irma knew that this would be a fight to the death.

Bloh Jobb made a grab for a letter opener that lay on his desk. Irma kicked at him and again missed by inches. Jobb moved towards the bathroom and found himself with his back to the wall and very little room to manoeuvre. He was trapped. As he searched for a way to avoid being killed, Irma advanced cautiously, waiting for him to make a lunge toward her. All she had to do was stick out her foot and he was dead. But he was fast with his hands too, and at all cost, she had to

173

avoid those. She had seen him with the Karate experts that he regularly flew in for exercise and knew how easily he killed them. His hands were deadly.

He made a sudden lunge. She lifted her foot, but the lunge was not for her, it was for her bull whip.

In one motion Bloh Jobb picked it up and lashed out at Irma, wrapping the whip around her neck. It was the last thing she felt. Bloh Jobb yanked it so hard that her neck broke, leaving her dead on her feet. Irma's body flew across the room with such force that she went right through the bathroom door and landed head first in the toilet. Cautiously, Jobb approached, making sure to stay away from the poisonous blades. There was no movement.

He flushed the toilet, which worked on a system of outside atmospheric air and water. It was of his own design, and to this date had never clogged. With some difficulty and loud gurgling sounds, Irma's body disappeared. Bloh Jobb could not resist a triumphant gloat: "Goodbye, Miss Klogg."

He calmly closed the demolished door and walked through to the large cabin in search of his cat.

Pussy Love and her daughter were still unconscious, curled up in their seats. This was good. He couldn't help thinking that he would like to be raped by her.

"Has anyone seen my cat?"

"I think I saw it under the seat by the cabin door," replied Dr. Yes.

"I haven't seen Irma," said Dr. Maybe. "Where did she go?"

"She's in the toilet...freshening up," said Bloh Jobb. "Ah, here is my kitty." He picked up his cat, but it was now only a stiff bundle of white fur. Rigor mortis was already setting in. Bloh Jobb let out a loud, gut-wrenching moan. Lifting the cat to his chest, he cradled it in his arms. "That fucking bitch! She killed my cat!"

"His cat's dead," said Dr. Maybe, as he watched Bloh

Jobb retire to his private cabin and slam the door after him.

"I wonder what he's going to do with it," said Dr. Yes. "I could do with a little cat*nip*. Get it? Huh?" Dr. Yes dug his elbow into his brother's side, pleased at his little joke, and just then the plane began to descend on its way to a final landing approach.

Chapter Fourteen

LONDON

The offices of British Special Intelligence were in a state of pandemonium. Information was coming in so fast from all around the world that P and his staff were pushed to the limit handling it. Telephones, telexes and computerized information transmitting systems were overloaded. P was trying to maintain a calm front, but he, too, was close to losing control. The only thing that stopped him from doing so was the surprising help he was getting from Bert Mummypenny, who, recognizing a crisis, threw deportment to the wind and took off his high heels, considerably speeding his movements around the office.

The red phone rang on P's desk. It was the Queen asking for another update. Her Royal Highness had been calling every half hour. Her concern was genuine: the economy of her kingdom was collapsing and she didn't know who was going to be able to polish her Crown Jewels.

As thousands more people stayed away from work by the minute, including members of the army and police forces, the criminal element amongst the population recognized an opportunity as never before. Those criminals who weren't taking the day off took to the streets, and robbery, looting, and other crimes ran rampant. It was the same in every industrialized nation, as confirmed by reports from around the world.

P picked up the phone. "Yes, Your Majesty....No, I have not found anyone to take over the cleaning of your Crown Jewels. Have you ever thought of doing them yourself?" P knew that he had overstepped his bounds the moment he spoke, but he didn't really care anymore.

"A queen simply doesn't do that sort of thing, P. May I remind you that you are one of the common people, P, and as such I can have your head cut off." P listened. He heard Her Majesty's hand being placed over the receiver, and muffled conversation. He assumed she was talking with her husband. She came back on the line. "Apparently, according to my husband, I'm not allowed to do that to commoners anymore."

"Well, that's very gratifying to know, Your Majesty."

"P, have you managed to track down the Prime Minister?"

"No, Your Majesty. With the limited forces still available, we have tried everything, but no trace of her yet. We do have one hope, however. According to the United States military attache stationed here in London, our agent, Triple 'O' Seven, survived an attack just outside Los Angeles and managed to capture an enemy agent called Pussy Love."

"Pussy Love?" said the Queen.

"Yes," said P. "We know that she was responsible for the death of a C.I.A. agent. But what alarms me is that no one except a few people, including Your Majesty, knew of Triple 'O' Seven's flight to Los Angeles."

"I hope, P, that you are not implying that the Queen of England is a spy."

"I am not implying anything at this point, Your Majesty." P gripped the red phone tighter. "I am simply stating a fact."

●

There were not many people on the streets of Waikiki to see the President and his men riding full gallop down Kalukaua Avenue, past the Outrigger and the Surfrider Hotels and onto the small adjacent street leading to Ala Wai Boulevard. It was an observation that Higgins shouted to the President as he struggled to keep up with him.

All the horses were tired and lathered. The healthiest looking animal was underneath One Finger In The Sky. The mule had the stamina to just keep going.

Arriving at the British Embassy, they dismounted near the edge of the manicured lawn and the President led the way to the front door.

"Great White Chief!" shouted One Finger In The Sky. "Death is in this house."

The words made everyone stand still. The President drew his pearl handled pistols from their holsters and went into a crouch position. His eyes narrowed, looking for danger. Seeing none, he turned to One Finger In The Sky.

"Why do you say such things, my fine feathered little red man? What great hunting signs tell you that there is death in this house?" Higgins already had out his note pad in anticipation of the President's next words. "Higgins, write that down, I ...."

"I have already written it down, in case you might want to say it again, Sir."

"Well?" asked the President, turning to One Finger In The Sky.

179

"The sign that tells me there is death in this house is the dead and bloody body that you, Great White Chief, are standing on."

The President looked down and then leapt away from the body. "Oh, grody!" said the President. Then, recovering: "Men, get your guns. We are going in."

The men rushed for their rifles. Keeping well back from the President, they followed after him as he ran for the entrance. With sixguns blazing, he stood in the entry way, shooting until his guns were empty. The men stood behind him in a clump, and once again caught up in the excitement of it all, started shooting as well. Although there was no one to be seen, they did an expert job of destroying the fine old English antique furniture. The President held up his hand to signal an end to the shooting.

Going from room to room, they discovered the dead bodies, some with their throats cut and lying in pools of congealed blood.

"It looks like we're too late, men," the President said. Higgins, get me P on the line. What in the hell is going on here?"

Higgins returned shortly, carrying a phone. "I have P on the line, Mr. President."

A red phone hung by its cord from the window of P's office on Picadilly Circus. Inside, P sat behind his desk with his ear to another phone.

"P, this is the President of the United States. I'm at the British Embassy in Hawaii. I need a description of those two agents. Everyone here has been killed."

P's ears began pounding. Hawaii? The whole staff killed? Wearily, he relayed a description of the two agents and waited for confirmation of their deaths.

Higgins was given the unpleasant task of trying to identify the bodies. He came back to the President with excitement in his voice. "Mr. President, they're not here, but come and look at this."

The President followed Higgins to the large wall map.

"Here, Sir. Look." Higgins pointed out the Marquesas Keys at the tip of Florida. "The coincidence is just too great. Sir, we were just at a bird sanctuary that was blown up, and look here. These islands are also in a national wildlife refuge, and they have been circled."

Not to be outdone and possibly lose his job with the Great White Chief, One Finger In The Sky came close to the map and stared intently.

"Well?" asked the President.

"It looks like fresh pencil to me, oh Great White Chief."

This was another golden opportunity for the President to make a decision of importance. He grabbed the phone. "P, it's the President. The agents must still be alive. They are, we think, heading for the Marquesas Keys, a group of small islands at the tip of Florida. We are on our way there now." The President turned to his men amid great excitement. All believed that these small islands were the answer to what was going on. "Men, we ride. Yahoo!"

The President ran outside to where the horses were waiting, and jumped onto his horse. He dug in his spurs, trying to get the horse onto its hind legs, but nothing happened. The President tried again, slapping the reins against each side of the horse's neck, but it stayed completely still.

"I think your horse is dead, Sir," Higgins said.

"Don't be ridiculous, Higgins. You can't ride a dead horse."

"That's what I was going to say, Sir." The President did not like the smug look on Higgins' face.

"Shit!" shouted the President, reluctantly getting off the horse. He looked around. Someone was going to have to give him a good, strong horse. He zeroed in on One Finger In The Sky, who stood quietly beside his mule.

One Finger In The Sky did not like the condescending smile that was on the Great White Cowboy's face. He had seen that same smile on other white men's faces all his life.

"Have you got any beads we can give this Indian for his horse?" whispered the President as he passed Higgins.

"No, Sir. No beads," came the reply.

"What else do Indians like?"

"You could try macadamia nuts, Sir. There's lots of them in Hawaii."

One Finger In The Sky also did not like the whispering that was going on. The President came up to him.

"My dear, red brother. I will speak to you as an equal." There was a solemn tone to the President's voice. "For many years throughout history, a great injustice has been done your people by the Great White Chief's government. I know that we have broken treaties that were made in good faith and should have been kept. I know that we have put your people into arid and unfertile areas of our great land and that many of them are starving and living in conditions that no one should live in."

One Finger In The Sky nodded in agreement. The President smiled. He was making good progress with the savage that stood before him.

"But, despite all these injustices, your people have stood proud. A symbol of the great American warrior. It didn't matter to you that we were victorious in mighty battles, that we killed your great fighting men, raped your women, and made a lot of money at the box office telling all about those things. You know why it didn't matter? Because you are above all that. You believe in things that are not important to the greedy white man. Do you know what I am saying?" The President placed both hands on One Finger In The Sky's shoulders and smiled at him.

"No," said One Finger In The Sky.

"What I am saying is that you will understand why the Great White Chief has to take your horse. Now do you understand?"

"You want my mule, Four Hooves on the Desert Sand?"

"Yes. What do you say, my faithful Indian companion."

"No," came the reply.

"Higgins, shoot him," the President said, standing back.

"That's not a good idea, Sir. We are holding up a lot of traffic."

The President looked down the avenue. It was true. There was a line of cars, and people were starting to get out, wondering what all the fuss was about.

The President turned around to One Finger In The Sky and poked his finger tips into the Indian's eyes. One Finger In The Sky staggered backwards and fell to the pavement in front of the first car. The President jumped on the mule and dug in his spurs. Four Hooves, not accustomed to such treatment, shot forward in terror. "Yeooo! Forward, men. We ride. Higgins, make sure that horse of mine is stuffed. If Roy Rogers can make a buck at it, I might be able to as well. And Higgins, make sure that Commie scum gets a pound or two of macadamia nuts. I don't want him coming back at me later."

Higgins was trying to write and mount his horse at the same time. He and the rest of the men roared off in pursuit of their Great White Chief.

The driver of the first car ran to help the old man who had fallen to the pavement. He grabbed the arm of One Finger In The Sky and helped him to his feet.

"Who was that masked man?" asked the driver.

"That's the fucking President of the United States," said One Finger In The Sky, giving the disappearing President one finger in the sky.

•

P was examining a large map of Florida. He quickly located the Marquesas Keys. He was excited. He tried to get more information from the President, but the line had gone dead. It was good that the President was on his way. He went to his window and hauled in the red phone, its receiver dangling from the long curly cord. He hesitated a second before interrupting.

"Your Majesty?"

As P was listening to her, Truscott and Bert Mummypenny came rushing into his office. P waved them to silence.

"Your Majesty, we have a break. Our agents have possibly found the H.Q. of what might be the enemy. They are on their way to Marquesas Keys, which is a small group of islands off the southernmost tip of Florida."

Truscott was trying to distract P, who finally put his hand over the mouthpiece and gave Truscott a chance to speak.

"We have found the Prime Minister and her husband!"

"Your Majesty, I'll get right back to you. Truscott of the Yard has just informed me that they have found the Prime Minister."

Chapter Fifteen

MARQUESAS KEYS

Seven islands make up the Marquesas Keys. Six of them are no more than small atolls, barely above the surface of the warm, crystal clear water that laps at their coral shores. The seventh island is, in contrast, quite large. Steep cliffs rise from small beaches on all sides. The huge imposing fortress-like compound at the centre of the island was obviously the headquarters of the fiend named Bloh Jobb.

A sleek speedboat landed and Triple 'O' Seven and Timmy Baby pulled it as far as possible up the beach of pure white sand. They checked their weapons silently, then slung them over their backs along with some extra belts of ammunition. They had a steep and difficult climb ahead of them.

"Don't forget to take your pills," joked Timmy.

Triple 'O' Seven fished in his pocket for the vial. There were about eight pills left. He was about to throw them away when, on impulse, he took all eight of them. Then he threw the empty vial on the sand.

"In for a penny, in for a pound," he muttered.

They made good progress up the first part of the steep cliff, but it was harder going nearer the top. A seagull resting on a ledge suddenly screamed and flew out at Triple 'O' Seven. He nearly lost his balance and fell on Timmy, who was right behind him.

It was extremely humid and sweat poured off them. Exhausted, they finally approached the last few feet before the top.

Triple 'O' Seven reached for a clump of scrub grass to pull himself up and over the edge of the cliff. As he grabbed the grass in his fist, a huge running shoe stamped down on his hand, making him scream with pain. Timmy, just below him, looked up in alarm.

"Hello there, Triple 'O' Seven. I have been expecting you." It was the black man with the white hands, the one they called Bloh Jobb.

Triple 'O' Seven looked up and was struck by the fanatical look in Jobb's eyes. He also noticed the dozen or so guards carrying sub-machine-guns pointed at him and Timmy Baby.

"It is Triple 'O' Seven, I presume?" The voice was mocking. "You are quite a man, Triple 'O' Seven. Very intriguing."

"How did you know that we were here? Who told you?"

"It was actually quite simple to predict your arrival. We knew the minute that you left Hawaii."

"Would you mind not standing on my hand? It hurts."

"Oh, yes. Of course. How rude of me. As I said, Triple 'O' Seven, you intrigue me. Please be my house guest." Bloh Jobb removed his foot from the hand, reached down and, with his immense strength, pulled Triple 'O' Seven to the top of the cliff. He shoved him towards the enormous house.

"You are forgetting my associate," said Triple 'O' Seven.

"Oh, yes, your associate. Unfortunately, he doesn't intrigue me as much as you." He signalled to one of the guards who still had his weapon trained on Timmy Baby. Triple 'O' Seven guessed what was going to happen and tried to get to the guard. Before he could, he was felled by the ham-like fist of Bloh Jobb. Stunned as he fell to the ground, he was still able to see the guard aim his weapon and unleash a burst of bullets. Triple 'O' Seven hoped he was not in for the same fate, or worse. He looked up at the murderous Bloh Jobb.

"The first opportunity I have, I'll kill you, Bloh Jobb."

Bloh Jobb let out a laugh, an evil, loud laugh. "I'm sure you will try, Triple 'O' Seven, and I will give you that opportunity soon enough. But first, why don't you come to the house and see what we are up to? After all the trouble you've gone to, and your delightful perseverance, you should, I feel, have some answers to all those questions I'm sure you have."

Aching from the climb and the blow to his head, Triple 'O' Seven went with Bloh Jobb and the guards. Soon they walked through a huge entry way and down along a high-ceilinged corridor.

"We have one of your friends here," said Bloh Jobb, opening a door. "You remember Pussy Love and her daughter?"

Triple 'O' Seven tried not to let any emotion show, but he knew that Jobb could see his relief.

"Ah! Fond of the little lady, huh?" laughed Bloh Jobb. "She was very useful to us as an assassin after we brainwashed her. We use a form of hypnotherapy. She will be useful to me again. As you can see, Triple 'O' Seven, she is undergoing a refresher course."

Pussy Love and her daughter were strapped into two chairs, with wires and electrodes attached to their heads. They looked like they were sleeping. A doctor was hovering over some machinery, monitoring needles that presumably showed brain waves.

"Come along, Triple 'O' Seven. I'm sure your curiosity is demanding more. Ah! Here we are."

They walked into a huge room which was almost three hundred feet long. Along one side of the wall was a bank of television screens spewing out data from different parts of the world. Below the screens was a glass-enclosed control room. To the left were about two dozen white-coated men looking into electron microscopes and another two dozen working with a huge molecular model. Guards were everywhere.

"Interesting, is it not?" said Bloh Jobb with a certain amount of pride in his voice.

"Yes. What is it?"

"Well, that's a long story, but very simply, it starts with the good Dr. Lawrence, whom one of my associates killed in London."

"That was the guy with his fingers and face eaten off. He was found with the prostitute in the back alley in Soho. But why kill him?"

"Dr. Lawrence was a brilliant man engaged in some very interesting research. He was working with an equally impressive group of scientists in France, also engaged in advanced research. Are you familiar with the Common Cold, Triple 'O' Seven? It is the product of a virus—a very simple organism, much smaller than bacteria, which multiplies uncontrollably in living organisms."

Bloh Jobb stepped up to the huge structure of yellow, green, and red balls stuck together by blue sticks. "How is your chemistry, Triple 'O' Seven? Perhaps you remember these molecular models from High School. A virus! Beautiful, don't you think? And there is one wonderful thing about viruses: they change, all the time. They *mutate*, if you like." Bloh Jobb held up his hands, then grabbed two of the spheres on the model and removed them. They were the size of basketballs. He stood back from the model.

"The flu, Triple 'O' Seven."

Bloh Jobb moved again to the model and put the two balls back in place. "And now, something completely new. A *new* virus, a *new* disease." Here, his voice rose. "And this new, mutant virus—Thank You, Dr. Lawrence!—is unstoppable! With a little effort and imagination, and my team of loyal doctors here, I came up with a marvellous idea, HAW-HAW!"

Triple 'O' Seven recoiled from the hearty laugh.

"Oh," said Bloh Jobb, his excitement quickly subsiding, "I'd like you to meet my associates, Dr. Yes and Dr. Maybe."

Triple 'O' Seven looked at the obviously gay albino and the fat Chinese man and tried to be funny. "Twins, I take it?" he asked Bloh Jobb. No one laughed; the three of them just looked at one another.

"How did you know?" said Bloh.

"Know what?" replied Triple 'O' Seven.

Jobb looked at him curiously, trying to figure out what Triple 'O' Seven really knew. He walked away, expecting Seven to follow him.

"The fat one is the one who ate Professor Lawrence. He's asked me to save you for a late lunch."

"Is that before or after you kill me?"

"I told him that it would be a cold meal. To continue, my team of doctors played around with it a little and we managed to mass produce the virus."

"Oh, my God! The production plant in Hawaii?"

"Ah! I see that you have put two and two together. Your little trip, which resulted in my factory being destroyed, was certainly an inconvenience, but it came a little too late. You see, we have distributed over two hundred million cans of the underarm deodorant through all of the economically powerful nations. What we did was put in a little aphrodisiac which made people want to do nothing but stay at home and screw, and that provided an ideal incubation period for the disease to take hold.''

''Christ! You mean to tell me that you have given over two hundred million people a cold?''

''No, you idiot! We have given them a new disease which renders them lethargic, unwilling to work, and, when combined with the aphrodisiac, makes them interested in only one thing!''

''You mean....''

Bloh Jobb was desperate for Triple 'O' Seven to see the genius of his plan, but he seemed to be taking an eternity. Just as Bloh Jobb was about to boil over, Seven finished his sentence.

''...sex?''

''Yes! Precisely. Their own pleasure, excluding everything else!'' Bloh Jobb shouted.

The implications were awesome, thought Triple 'O' Seven. Two hundred million people interested in sex. ''You mean to tell me two hundred million people...?''

''You've got it,'' screamed Bloh Jobb. Then, calmer: ''Actually, the number is approaching three hundred million by now. Courtesy of the greatest selling force in the world.''

''The Girl Guides!''

''Exactly. Of course, there's a much better markup in viruses than in cookies and almond-covered chocolates, but they have no idea what's going on. As a result, many countries are now on the verge of chaos. Looting, murder and total economic collapse will follow.''

''That's disgusting,'' said Triple 'O' Seven.

''Thank you,'' said Bloh Jobb, happy that he had shocked the British agent with his dastardly scheme.

''Using the Girl Guides like that. Have you no scruples?''

''No. Let me add one essential detail. My team here has made a medical breakthrough and we now have the only cure available. Within the next thirty minutes, we will inform the world of their predicament. Look at the screens along that wall, Triple 'O' Seven. You can see the unrest and turmoil is worldwide. They have only fragments of industries, armies and navies left. They can do nothing. My own people are ready to take over the governments of each country. There's also another wrinkle in the scheme of things. See this satellite transmitter? It's already in a countdown phase. Twenty-six minutes to go. Into each aerosol can, we put a small radio device and an even smaller, but very, very powerful, bomb. Enough to wipe out a block of buildings or two.

"In twenty-six minutes, we will begin to selectively explode those three hundred million cans just to show the power that we have. Of course, if the country we pick on, and the first two are England and the United States, wants to meet our terms, then we can do some business."

"And what are your terms?" asked Triple 'O' Seven. He was stalling for time. He had to think. There were only twenty-four minutes to go.

"Total submission. All the country's money and complete control over its weapons and forces. You see, Triple 'O' Seven, I really am going to be master of the world."

Bloh Jobb led him out of the huge room and into the private gymnasium that would become an arena of death for Triple 'O' Seven. Apart from all of the normal equipment such as weights, gymnastic apparatus and benches, the walls were covered with a variety of lethal weapons. Spears, chains with spiked balls, knives, clubs and cudgels filled one wall. In the corner was a stereo system with two huge speakers and a rack of popular aerobic-disco type records.

"Well, I hope your curiosity has been satisfied, Triple 'O' Seven. This is where I work out. I'm afraid the time has come for me to kill you. My own curiosity compels me to find out if you have any perseverance in fighting for your life, or if your tracking me down was a fluke.''

Triple 'O' Seven swallowed. His throat was very dry. Bloh Jobb had taken off his shirt to reveal one of the most massive, most impressive muscular bodies that he had ever seen.

''Choose your weapon, Triple 'O' Seven. Anything you like.''

Seven went over to the razor sharp spears. He selected a medium sized one and pulled it from the wall.

''Ah! An excellent choice. Throw it anytime you like. Don't mind me while I warm up. Normally it would be your privilege to choose a popular song to exercise to,'' Jobb said, walking over to the stereo, ''but I'm in a particularly good mood and I must insist.''

Bloh Jobb put a record on and a loud Bumpa-Bumpa-Bumpa sound came blasting out from the speakers, filling the gymnasium. It reminded Triple 'O' Seven of the exercise program he enjoyed watching on television. Bloh Jobb was going through a series of stretching exercises that looked like some form of yoga.

Triple 'O' glanced at his watch. Only fifteen minutes away from detonation of the cans. He got as close to Jobb as he felt was safe. The black monster was too calm, too confident, and Triple 'O' Seven felt uneasy. He threw the spear as hard as he could. In a blur of movement, Bloh Jobb spun around twice on the balls of his feet. On the first spin, he caught the spear; on the second, he threw it back at Triple 'O' Seven so hard that Triple 'O' barely managed to duck. The spear was thrown with such tremendous force that it made a whistling sound as it passed Triple 'O' Seven and buried itself into the wall behind him. The shaft of the spear had almost disappeared.

Bloh Jobb went back to his stretching exercises. ''Take off your coat and relax. Try to do better than that, Triple 'O' Seven. I know you can. I would be very disappointed if that was your best effort. There's nothing I would like more than to keep the fat man waiting for his dinner.''

''My sentiments, exactly,'' said Triple 'O' Seven. He took the advice and removed his jacket. He was stunned by the speed with which Bloh Jobb had moved. This would be harder than he thought.

''I wonder if you'd be good enough to turn off that damn music,'' Triple 'O' said. ''I find it hard to think.''

Jobb laughed, moved to the stereo, and gently removed the record. ''Maybe you should try a lighter spear. It might be easier for you to throw.''

''Thank you for the suggestion. I think I will.'' Triple 'O' Seven took one of the smaller spears from the wall and looked for a better position in the gymnasium. He was close to a vaulting box. If Bloh Jobb did the same thing again, he would be able to dive behind it for cover.

Triple 'O' Seven wondered if a question might distract the big man enough for him to gain an advantage. ''Who is the spy who's been feeding you information about every move I make?'' Moving with lightning speed, he threw the second spear as hard as he could. Bloh Jobb caught it effortlessly, but this time only used one spin to throw it back. It penetrated through both sides of the vaulting box with the razor sharp blade sticking out where Triple 'O' Seven would have been, if he'd had the chance to dive there.

''It's a good job you didn't dive behind that for cover, Triple 'O' Seven,'' laughed Bloh Jobb. ''I think you would have been quite dead.''

''I would agree with you,'' said Triple 'O' Seven.

''In answer to your question, I think you would be very surprised. Let's see now. There's your boss, P; his secretary, and of course, there's Truscott of Scotland Yard. Then of course, there is the Prime Minister; and then there is always the Queen. Don't you have any idea at all?''

''If I did, I wouldn't ask. Can you suggest what I should try next in the way of weapons?'' Triple 'O' Seven looked at his watch as he turned back to the wall of weapons. Eleven minutes to go.

"Why don't you try the chain with the two sticks at each end? It's a favorite of mine," replied Bloh Jobb. "The prime target, as you must know, is the neck, groin or legs. And, of course, you have to get a little closer to your intended victim." Bloh Jobb was still going through his stretching exercises. "I'm nearly through warming up. When I'm finished, we can get down to a serious workout."

Bloh Jobb was thoroughly enjoying the situation. Triple 'O' Seven was obviously inferior to him physically. It would be like a cat playing with a mouse. He thought about his cat. Yes. He would toss this mouse around for a while before completely breaking every bone in its body. It would be fun.

Triple 'O' Seven took down the suggested weapon, which was used specifically in Oriental martial arts. He was familiar with it, but not very good at using it. His mother had explained it to him many years ago and, used properly, it was deadly. Triple 'O' tried to remember some of the moves, but only twisted the twirling bone-hard handles around his arms and made a fool of himself. Jobb was laughing. Triple 'O' Seven thought that he had distracted him and let the weapon fly. If one of the handles hit him anywhere around the head, he might stand a chance.

Bloh Jobb just laughed louder. With a quick step to one side, he caught the flying chain and proceeded to show Triple 'O' Seven how it was done.

"Concentration, Triple 'O' Seven. Concentration. That's the secret to this weapon. See how fast it moves?" The chains made a whirring noise as the handles flew so fast they could hardly be seen. Bloh Jobb suddenly let the weapon go. Before Seven had the chance to move, the chains were about his ankles and he was thrown to the floor. The hard wooden handles hit him on the shins, and he screamed in pain. It felt like his legs were being cut off with a hack saw.

"Concentration and practice, Triple 'O' Seven. That's what it takes to use that weapon. Choose another one."

Triple 'O' Seven, writhing with pain, struggled to be free of the chains. They were so tight that the circulation to his feet was cut off. When he finally did remove it from around his ankles, he pulled down his socks to see a stream of blood running down each leg from the broken, swollen skin.

"You have ruined a very good pair of socks," said Triple 'O' Seven.

"I'm glad you still have a sense of humour, Triple 'O' Seven. Nothing quite like a bit of gay repartee before dinner."

"What weapon do you suggest this time?" asked Triple 'O' as he staggered to his feet. The pain was excruciating. The blood running into his shoes was warm and sticky.

"Why don't you choose," Jobb said.

"All right, I will. It's almost like choosing a wine to go with dinner, isn't it? This looks like a very good year for steel. I think I'll take this." Triple 'O' Seven took a large jungle knife off the wall. He was not going to throw it this time. This time, he would wait for Bloh Jobb to come to him. Only nine minutes left.

"Oh! I see that you want me to get down to business. My compliments on making a good choice, Triple 'O' Seven. I have gouged out many an eye with that knife. Maybe I should show you how it's done. One quick flick of the tip and bingo. The eye just pops right out."

Bloh Jobb advanced and Triple 'O' Seven retreated. This man was very quick on his feet, probably a master at most of the Oriental forms of martial arts. His one chance was to get in close and hope that he could stick in the knife. What a mismatch!

"You can only retreat so far, Triple 'O' Seven."

"It's my family motto," Triple 'O' Seven replied. "We never retreat until the enemy advances."

195

"Very amusing." Bloh Jobb projected himself so quickly through the air that Triple 'O' Seven was caught completely by surprise. In one motion, Jobb's foot kicked the knife out of his hand and continued on to slam him in the windpipe, making Triple 'O' Seven gasp for breath. Bloh Jobb picked up the knife and replaced it on the wall. "I will pluck out your eyes later, Triple 'O' Seven, but first I will give you a lesson in the art of how to kill a man slowly."

Bloh Jobb spun on his heel and caught Triple 'O' Seven in the ribs. The force of the kick sent Triple 'O' Seven rocketing back over the vaulting box and up against the wall.

"Oh, really now, Triple 'O' Seven, surely you can do better than that. At least try to hit me once before I pluck out your eyes with the knife." Bloh Jobb picked up Triple 'O' as if he was an empty potato sack and held him against the wall. "Come now, Triple 'O' Seven, maybe a couple of slaps will revive you." With that, Jobb let loose a vicious backhand slap that made Triple 'O' Seven's senses reel.

Seven again gasped for breath. He was helpless, his throat raw. He barely managed to make a 'T' shape with his hands, indicating a time out. Bloh Jobb's response was to throw him across the room with such force that the wind was knocked from him as he crashed against the far wall.

"What's the matter, Triple 'O' Seven? You want a little rest? You want to avoid the pain of your eyes being plucked from their sockets? You have nice eyes, too. The fat man will love them...as an appetizer for the main course."

"I just need a glass of water. How can I give you a fight when my throat is like this," croaked Triple 'O' Seven.

"The water fountain is behind you. By all means, have as much water as you like."

Triple 'O' Seven struggled to his feet, and staggered over to the water fountain. He pushed the stainless steel button and bent his head to the flow of ice cold water. Only seven minutes to go. The water poured down his throat. Still struggling to keep his balance, he turned to face Bloh Jobb, and noticed him choosing one of the spears on the wall.

"Which one do you think I should use to start off with?" asked Jobb.

Triple 'O' Seven shook his head. Something was happening. The dizziness had disappeared and in its place was a state of euphoria. Total calmness and a feeling of well-being surged through his body. There was no more pain.

The pills! The God-damned pills were finally working. All he had needed to do was to take them with water! Of course! He started to laugh.

Bloh Jobb turned to face him. "Ah! Hysteria. It's a common reaction amongst those who are about to die. I was asking you, Triple 'O' Seven, to assist me in choosing a spear."

"Take the big one, you monster."

Bloh Jobb chose the big spear and hefted it in his huge hands. "Getting in the last insult, eh? Well, I must say that you have disappointed me tremendously. In doing so, you have reduced this little exercise to nothing more than a waste of time. Goodbye, Triple 'O' Seven." He hurled the spear straight for Triple 'O' Seven's chest.

Still laughing, Triple 'O' saw the weapon hurtling towards him. The strange thing was that it appeared to be moving in slow motion. Without stopping his laughter, Triple 'O' Seven caught the spear, as Bloh Jobb had done earlier. He spun around on the balls of his feet and threw the spear back at his assailant. The spear would have passed through a lesser man. As it was, the blade caught the shocked Bloh Jobb slightly off guard, nicked his arm and caused a trickle of blood to drip from the wound.

"Try two at once," suggested Triple 'O' Seven, chuckling. "Maybe the fat man out there can have someone else for supper? I see I have drawn blood."

Bloh Jobb was still in a state of shock. No one had ever done this to him. But his surprise was soon replaced by

197

controlled rage. He selected two spears with barbed blades and flung them as hard as he could at Triple 'O' Seven.

"Can't you do better than that?" said Triple 'O' Seven, catching the spears easily. "Let me show you how it's done." With a flick of his arm so fast it was difficult to see, the spears whistled back at Bloh Jobb and pierced the wall on both sides of his head.

For the first time in his life, a flicker of fear showed in Bloh Jobb's eyes. His stomach knotted.

"Well, this is getting very tiresome," Triple 'O' said, advancing on Bloh Jobb. "I'm afraid I have to bring this to an end. You obviously seem to favour unarmed combat, so why don't we see what you're made of?"

Bloh Jobb rushed at him with a flying kick. Again, to Triple 'O' Seven it looked like slow motion. He ducked and spun on his heel, kicking Jobb on the side of the head as he passed. Bloh Jobb fell into some weight equipment, and sent it scattering in all directions. He picked up a heavy bar bell weight and threw it at Triple 'O' Seven. Seven flew into the air, screaming with a high kick. The cast iron weight split in two, like a piece of dry wood.

Bloh Jobb pulled the chain with the wooden handles from the rack behind him and spun the weapon at Triple 'O' Seven's throat. Triple 'O' caught the weapon easily, without even breaking stride. He gave his opponent a spectacular display of how to twirl the weapon around. "Concentration, Bloh Jobb. Concentration is what you need to use this weapon."

Sheer terror filled the eyes of Bloh Jobb. What had happened? He didn't know. What kind of devil was this?

Triple 'O' Seven let the weapon fly back at Bloh Jobb. It moved so fast through the air that Bloh Jobb didn't even have a chance to react. The chain snapped around his neck with so much force that it lifted him off his feet and hurled him backwards to the two spears stuck in the gymnasium wall behind him. Its wooden handles wrapped around the spears and held him suspended. The last thing that Bloh Jobb saw was Triple 'O' Seven throwing in rapid succession the six remaining spears. They passed through Bloh Jobb and pinned him to the wall.

Triple 'O' Seven looked at the grisly sight in front of him. "Dinner is served. I wonder if the fat man would like a fondue?"

He looked at his watch. Four minutes to go.

Chapter Sixteen

LONDON

"Where did you find the Prime Minister?"

"We found her and her husband in a hunting lodge in Scotland. Both of them were unconscious."

"Is she all right?" asked P.

"I'm afraid not, P," said Truscott. "It appears they overdosed on sex. Her husband is in pretty poor shape, but he should be all right. They have put him in an iron lung."

"My God!" exclaimed P.

"Well, I'm afraid that's not the worst of it, P. The doctors examining the Prime Minister found a complete lack of motivation. She has absolutely no desire to govern the country. And funnily enough, the first three doctors we asked had absolutely no desire to examine her."

"What's wrong with her, then?"

"She has been diagnosed as having a new type of virus, a mutant virus, if you like."

"How ghastly! A virus! You mean like the flu? Do you realizing what you are saying, Truscott? Are you saying that anyone can catch this virus and be left with absolutely no desire to go to work?" P stopped short and raised an eyebrow. It suddenly occurred to him that his job hadn't been much fun lately. He looked over Truscott's head and saw Bert Mummypenny bustle past the open doorway to his office. P's eyes widened.

Truscott squirmed in his chair. P snapped out of it and began to pace around the room at breakneck speed. He stopped and looked at Truscott.

"What's the sex angle on this?"

"Apparently, in the initial phase of this new disease, the victim has only a single, unwavering desire. An incredible, overpowering urge to...."

Truscott was cut off by a horrified cry from P. "Fuck! The Queen!" P jumped for the red phone, which connected him directly to the Palace.

"Hello."

"Your Majesty," said P, recognizing the clipped tone. "I want you to tell me if you have...ahem!...have you and the Royal Prince been...engaging in...."

"What?"

"I need to know, Your Majesty, whether or not you and the Prince have been...involved...romantically. Recently, that is."

"Who is this? Are you some sort of heavy breather?"

"It's P, Your Majesty."

The hand went over the mouthpiece and P heard the Queen speak to her husband.

"Darling, do put down that model airplane. P wants to know if we've been having it off lately. What shall I tell him?"

P waited for her reply.

"He says he can't remember," the Queen said. "I vaguely

202

recall something in Scotland, about twelve months ago."

"Ah, I see," said P, visibly relieved. "That is excellent news. I will keep you informed, Your Majesty." He hung up the phone.

The phones in the office were quiet for a moment. P sat and thought. Truscott quietly left the room. Where did this virus come from? How could it spread so rapidly? He'd never heard of the flu or the Common Cold reaching such enormous proportions. And was there a cure...? P suddenly thought of the dead Professor Lawrence.

He had to speak to Triple 'O' Seven. And now a horrible thought entered his head. There was something drastically wrong. Ever since he had engaged Triple 'O' Seven in this mission, the enemy had been one step ahead of him. First in Calico, then Hawaii, and if things came in threes, Triple 'O' was probably being set up in this group of islands off the tip of Florida.

P slammed his fist on the desk. There was a spy leaking information. But who the hell was it? The Prime Minister; Truscott; Bert Mummypenny? The President?

He thought the whole thing through and checked what he himself had done. Had he inadvertently led Triple 'O' Seven into danger? God-damn it! He slammed the desk again.

"Mizzzz Mummypenny, get me the Admiralty." He went to the blue phone. Admiral Pelican came on the line. "Hello, Percy. P here. Listen, do we have any ships in the Gulf of Mexico? I need a favour."

•

Triple 'O' Seven looked at his watch. It was very close to the deadline. In less than three minutes, Bloh Jobb's organization would demonstrate their awesome power, and those twins, Yes and Maybe, would unleash their ultimatum to the world. He opened the door of the gymnasium and ran

203

down the short corridor. Two guards saw him coming and tried to raise their weapons. Triple 'O' Seven was faster and quickly dispatched them, taking both of their sub-machine-guns.

Kicking open the door to the operations room, he leapt in and fired bursts from both guns. Everyone headed for cover, Dr. Maybe and Dr. Yes leading the way.

"Oh no! That's my dinner that's shooting at us," said Dr. Yes.

"Obviously your dinner doesn't agree with you," answered Dr. Maybe as he crawled for the heavier cover of a large workbench. "Let's get out of here. If he killed Bloh Jobb, I'm not staying around to let him have a go at me."

Both brothers took a quick look over the top of the bench to see where Triple 'O' Seven was. He was still some distance from them and hiding behind other work benches in the room as the guards, over their initial surprise, started to return his fire.

A bullet tugged at Triple 'O' Seven's sleeve. Whirling, he fired at a guard who had managed to get behind him somehow. His bullets found their mark and the guard crumpled to the ground.

Triple 'O' Seven worked his way towards the glass control room. On the wall above the control room the bank of television screens showed the satellite uplink zeroing in on a transponder which would in turn relay the message back to earth and detonate the bombs in the underarm deodorant spray cans. He had to reach the booth where white-coated men were working frantically to align the two units. He could also see a large digital readout clock of the time remaining. Two minutes, ten seconds.

He sprayed the control room with a shower of bullets to distract the technicians in the booth. But the control room was protected with thick bullet-proof glass and the bullets had no effect whatsoever. The three technicians remained at their posts.

Analyzing the situation, he reasoned that the weakest part of the control room was the door. Triple 'O' Seven made his way there as fast as he could. Keeping an eye out behind him, he saw the guards closing in. He turned and swept the room with bullets. The coloured balls of the large molecular model shattered and flew into a million pieces as the guards dove for cover.

Worming his way towards the control room door, he noticed a large steel refrigeration unit containing the vaccine for the mutant virus. The last thing he wanted was the contents destroyed. Thank God no one had yet thought to destroy it and thereby ensure the total collapse of the world economy, thought Triple 'O'. He looked up again at the digital clock.

One minute, ten seconds.

Triple 'O' Seven rose from the floor and sprinted for the control room door amid a vicious hail of fire. He aimed one of his machine guns at the door lock and pulled the trigger but nothing happened. The gun was empty. Quickly, he aimed the other gun and shot off the lock. With a kick, the door opened and he was inside the control room.

Two of the three men turned from the controls with pistols aimed at Triple 'O' Seven. They lost the draw and as bullets pierced their bodies they fell backwards over the controls.

"Deactivate, or you're dead!" shouted Triple 'O' Seven to the remaining technician, who still stood with his back to Triple 'O', intent on the control board. Triple 'O' Seven saw from the bank of television screens that the alignment of the uplink and the transponder was almost complete.

When the time-clock hit zero, unparalleled devastation would occur. He had to reach the red deactivate button to the right of the man in front of him. Fifty seconds left.

"For the last time!" he barked.

As the man turned around, the blood drained from Triple 'O' Seven's face.

"Hi!" said Timmy, a smile on his face.

"Timmy? But I thought you were dead."

"They had to make you think that, don't you see?"

"You mean...?"

"Sorry, pal. It really was a lot of fun working with you."

Fifteen seconds left.

The sudden realization that Timmy was the man providing the information to Bloh Jobb left a hollow, tight feeling in Triple 'O' Seven's stomach. His thoughts raced. Of course! Timmy had met him in L.A. and been with him every step of the way since. It explained why Bloh Jobb had always been one move ahead of him.

"I'm sorry, too, Timmy. You know what I have to do."

Six seconds.

"Go ahead. If you can."

Three seconds.

Triple 'O' Seven squeezed the trigger and Timmy flew backwards. The bullets made a popping sound as they tore through his body. Shoving past the body, Triple 'O' Seven slammed down on the button and with just one second showing on the clock, everything came to a standstill. He looked at the lifeless body sprawled over the control panel. It was not a pretty sight.

Triple 'O' Seven turned his attention to the guards now outside the booth. He could see the fat Chinese man and the albino running out the door. The guards had the control booth surrounded with guns raised, waiting for him to come out. Triple 'O' Seven checked his weapon. There was probably no more than a dozen rounds left. Looking around the booth, he picked up the two pistols from the dead men and stuck them in his belt.

He was trapped. There was no way out except through the door. With fifty or more armed guards out there, he had no chance at all. If that was the way it had to be, he thought, he would take as many of them with him as he could. With machine gun in one hand and pistol in the other, he headed for the door. The guards all raised their weapons, ready to fire.

As Triple 'O' Seven burst out of the door, he heard the strangest shouts from the far end of the enormous room.

"Charge! Charge!" yelled the President of the United States. With sixguns blazing, he galloped in at full speed, followed by Higgins and his faithful companions. "Giddy up there, Two Hooves in the Sky or whatever your name is." The mule snorted and bellowed beneath him as it ran around the room. The President kicked one of the guards as he rode by and slashed at another with his pistol.

Triple 'O' Seven watched as the horsemen rode around the room led by a strange-looking man in a tattered blue satin shirt with what looked like the remains of white fringes hanging from its sleeves. Soot around his eyes gave him the appearance of wearing a mask.

The President rode up to Triple 'O' Seven. "From what I've been told, you must be Triple 'O' Seven."

"Yes, I am."

"Pretty good timing for a rescue, huh?" said the President. He seemed oblivious to the bullets flying around the room.

"Perfect."

"Comes from my movie background. Timing is everything in the movies. Remember that, son, and don't forget to see my next movie."

"Movie?"

"Yes, I'm going to put all this into a movie. Working title right now is *Bonzo Goes Ape*. What do you think?"

"Sounds great. I wouldn't miss it."

"Good," said the President. "Well, if you'll excuse me, I have to go and finish this up." With that, he adjusted himself in the saddle and looked over the battle scene. He chose a target and spurred the mule towards a group of guards.

"Hi, I'm Higgins, glad to meet you, Triple 'O' Seven. You have led us on quite a chase. What's going on here?"

Triple 'O' Seven quickly filled him in and pointed out where the vaccine cabinet was. "By the way, who was that masked man?"

"That is the fucking President of the United States of America," said Higgins, with a real ring of pride in his voice.

Triple 'O' Seven looked out over the room. The President had his mule up on its hind legs, its front legs slashing the air and hitting the heads of the guards. He waved his arm at Higgins and looked as though he was really enjoying himself. Higgins was enjoying this, too. Maybe if he played his cards right, he could be in the President's next movie.

Triple 'O' Seven still had work to do, even though everything seemed to be under control. He ran to the end of the room, down the corridor, and into the room where Pussy Love and her daughter were being held. They were alone but still unconscious and hooked up to the electrodes. Triple 'O' Seven pulled the mass of wires from their heads and as he did so, they awoke, startled.

"Are you all right?"

"Yes, I think so." Pussy Love shook her head vigorously, trying to remove the sleep from her brain. She reached for her daughter.

Triple 'O' Seven marvelled at her beauty. She seemed to have no trace of the brainwashing left in her. He knew he was in love and wanted to take care of them both. Grabbing her hand, he said, "Come on, we have to get out of here." He opened the door slowly.

Dr. Yes and Dr. Maybe were still around somewhere, and must be considered dangerous. He did not wish to be surprised at this stage of the game. He led Pussy Love and her daughter out of the building. There was no sign of the twins.

They found an easier way to scramble down the cliff to the

beach where the boat had been left. Lifting the little girl into the boat, he and Pussy Love struggled to launch the boat into the clear, warm water. As soon as they were clear of the sand, he helped Pussy Love in and climbed on board himself.

The engine caught with a roar and the boat surged torward the mainland. Triple 'O' Seven took a long look at Pussy Love, her blonde hair flying in the warm breeze. Her short, clinging dress had gotten wet in the surf, further emphasizing her perfect breasts and hard nipples.

"They're beautiful," shouted Triple 'O' Seven.

Pussy Love turned and smiled at him.

"Listen," said Triple 'O', "I know we haven't really gotten to know one another, but will you marry me?"

"I thought you'd never ask. I fell in love with you the minute your chocolate gun melted. Thank you for rescuing me and my daughter. And the answer is yes."

"Yahoo!" shouted Seven. All three of them laughed.

Triple 'O' Seven had never been happier, and as they raced across the water, no words were spoken. The spray and the wind on his face had a refreshing sting to it.

Suddenly, his reverie was shaken by a strange noise. He looked around. Above and behind him he saw the grinning faces of Dr. Yes and Dr. Maybe in the plastic bubble of a small helicopter. They had launched a heat-seeking rocket at the boat! Triple 'O' cranked the wheel hard right and stared back in horror at the blurred snout of the missile slicing through the water behind them. As he reached for Pussy Love and Kitty in a desperate attempt to save them his hands left the wheel and the boat took a sudden lurch. Triple 'O' felt himself thrown overboard. Pussy lunged for the wheel and looking back, her eyes met Triple 'O' Seven's. Then Pussy gunned the engine and veered away. The wake of the speedboat swept over Seven's head, and when he bobbed to the surface he saw the boat explode in a great ball of fire.

The water was so clear, and as the helicopter made a pass

over the burning remains of the boat, the twins could see nothing but scattered debris floating on the surface of the ocean.

The little girl's doll was torn and ripped. It bobbed gently on the waves, but the burned and unseeing glass eyes looked up at the evil faces of Dr. Yes and Dr. Maybe.

"There goes a perfectly good dinner," said Dr. Yes, and the helicopter soared away from the carnage toward the mainland. The brothers had many new schemes in mind.

Epilogue

LONDON

It was almost summer. The streets still thronged with businessmen in three-piece suits but the women wore colourful light summer dresses. There was an air of optimism once again. The country had been close to disaster, but the vaccine had been flown in as soon as possible by the President and people started to return to work as the disease left their bodies. It had been a close call. Some problems remained, including what to do with the unemployed underarm deodorant factory workers.

The President of the United States was taking full advantage of his part in the victory and was already in pre-production on a film based on the story. He was negotiating with a late night talk show host to play him in the movie. Higgins had been cast as One Finger in the Sky and was living on an Indian reserve in Arizona, preparing for the role.

At British Intelligence, P wasn't sure whether he was a

hero or a scapegoat. The ship that Admiral Percy Pelican had sent had opened fire on the wrong island. P was taking the blame for that.

Discovering their mistake, the Royal Navy vessel had promptly steamed to the next island and blasted the hell out of it until they found out that it, too, was the wrong island. Again, P took the blame.

The third time, they were lucky. They found the right island. However, on their way there, they came across the burned remains of a speedboat with three bodies floating in the water. The little girl and the woman known as Pussy Love were dead.

Triple 'O' Seven would have been dead, too, but Pussy Love had driven the boat just far enough away from him. The last effects of the pills had allowed him to withstand the tremendous shock wave that followed the explosion and enabled him to tread water for three hours. Triple 'O' Seven was lucky to have been found and fished from the water. He would have drowned soon. P was taking credit for finding Triple 'O' Seven and for solving the crisis. He didn't know if that credit belonged to him or not, but he would take it anyway.

The Prime Minister's sex spree in Scotland was kept secret, and she was able to recover her iron will and return to governing the country. The Queen had hired the Prime Minister's husband to polish her Crown Jewels; he was capable of little else.

The buzzer sounded on P's desk. It was Bert Mummy-penny. ''Triple 'O' Seven is on his way up.''

It was the first time that P had seen Triple 'O' since the crisis began. He had spent a long time in hospital recuperating from his ordeal. He had also been very depressed over the death of Pussy Love and her daughter. When Triple 'O'

Seven left the hospital, he went to visit his mother, Anastasia Klause. He spent two weeks with her. P didn't know what they discussed and preferred not to know. He only knew Triple 'O' had shed a lot of tears over the deaths of Pussy Love and Kitty.

P pulled a cheque from underneath his desk calendar, and looked at it. He considered that Triple 'O' Seven had earned every penny.

In the street below, a Rolls Royce pulled up outside the newsstand that was in reality the secret entrance to British Intelligence. Triple 'O' Seven got out and stretched his legs. Not wasting any time, he walked over to the blind man and kicked him in the groin. As the man doubled over, Seven brought up his knee and sent the blind man crashing through the plate glass window. Without stopping, he walked through the shop and into the elevator which took him up to see P.

"Ah, Mizzz Mummypenny. How are you?"

Bert lowered his thick false eyelashes, fluttering them as he did so. "Fine, thank you. Good to see you."

"Would you please ask P not to test me with any more blind men, downstairs."

"What blind man?"

"The one I just knocked through the plate glass window."

"P didn't put him there. I'm afraid it must have been a real blind man."

"Oh...well then, there's been a terrible accident downstairs."

"When are we going to have that drink after work?" flirted Bert, changing the subject.

"I'm afraid it won't be for a while. I am off to Monte Carlo this afternoon." Triple 'O' Seven saw the disappointment in Bert's face. "But we'll have a drink as soon as I get back."

Bert smiled. "Let me take your hat and coat," he offered.

"No thanks, let me see if I can get it right this time." Triple 'O' Seven threw his hat and coat towards the stand, but as before, they went out the window. "One of these days," sighed Triple 'O' Seven, and he walked into P's office.

"Glad to see you, Triple 'O' Seven," said P. He rose from his desk and shook his hand. "I can't thank you enough for what you did. Oh, by the way, here is the cheque for the two hundred thousand pounds we promised you."

"But you already gave me a hundred thousand."

"Consider it a bonus from a very grateful government. Sit down."

There was an infernal noise coming from Picadilly Circus. P leaned his head out the window. "Great Scott! Another huge pile-up. What asshole caused it this time?" He looked at the tangle of cars piled up around the statue of Eros and slammed down the window, shook his head and settled back into his chair.

P's face became sombre. "My deep regrets, Triple 'O' Seven, concerning Miss Love and her daughter."

"Thank you, Sir."

P returned to his normal brusque manner. "I thought you might like to know, we've found out that Timmy Baby was a traitor from the very beginning. He was in the Soho area around the time of Professor Lawrence's murder, and he certainly fingered his fellow CIA agent, Joseph Martini, in Los Angeles. He would have done his best to try to destroy you eventually."

Triple 'O' Seven took the news quietly.

"Naturally," P continued, "we were curious about his connection with this Bloh Jobb fellow.... Have you ever heard of a woman named Irma Klogg?"

"A ladies' shoe designer?" offered Triple 'O' Seven.

"You might say that. She was closely associated with a certain General Bretzky, top man of Russian Intelligence. In any case, Irma Klogg has disappeared into thin air, but we *have* managed to discover Timmy Baby's real name: Timmy Baby Klogg."

Triple 'O' Seven's face registered surprise.

"He was the son of Irma Klogg. Quite tragic, really...."

Triple 'O' Seven nodded his agreement. P looked at Triple 'O' and seemed to want to say something more, but instead he coughed, rose from his chair, and came around from behind the desk.

"You did a fine job, Triple 'O' Seven." They shook hands, and P went back to his chair. "Well, where are you off to now?"

"I'm heading for Monte Carlo to spend some of this money and catch a little sun," said Triple 'O' Seven.

"Good. Is there anything else I can do for you?"

"Yes, there is," Triple 'O' said. "The moment you learn the whereabouts of Dr. Maybe and Dr. Yes, I want to be notified." Triple 'O' Seven walked to the door. "I mean it, P. I want to be the first to know." His voice had a hard edge that P had never heard before. "I have a score to settle."

Directive to All Readers

MISSION:

CONTINUE TO ENJOY AND LAUGH. LAUGHTER
IS NATURE'S BEST WEAPON AGAINST ALL THE
BAD THINGS IN THIS WORLD.

MISSION:

LOOK FORWARD TO NEXT TOP SECRET BOOK
WHEN AGENT TRIPLE 'O' SEVEN TRIES TO
AVENGE THE DEATHS OF PUSSY LOVE AND
KITTY.

MISSION:

DO NOT REVEAL CONTENTS OF FIRST BOOK.

MISSION:

CONTACT WRITER AT PUBLISHER'S OFFICE TO
ORDER VAST QUANTITIES OF TRIPLE 'O'
SEVEN BOOKS.

MISSION:

SEE THE UPCOMING FILM OF THIS TOP
SECRET FILE.

MISSION ACCOMPLISHED.